FLOWER PHANTOMS

Sir Arthur Ronald Fraser was born in 1888, the fourth son of an Inverness-shire cloth merchant who had moved to London. Fraser had a conventional education at St. Paul's School, but by his early teens was writing poetry, which was published in the *Westminster Gazette*, much to his family's amusement. At eighteen he was put to work in an insurance company, but in his spare time read at the British Museum; he was particularly interested in Buddhism. He served in the First World War and was in the trenches by November 1914. He was seriously wounded at the battle of Beaumont-Hamel and invalided out. He made his career in the overseas section of the Department of Trade, and in the Foreign Office, serving in Argentina and France as the Commercial Minister in the British Embassies there, and later as a Government Director of the Suez Canal, when he was resident in Egypt. His knighthood in 1949 was one of several decorations in recognition of a distinguished diplomatic career. He published twenty-seven novels between 1924 and 1961 and in later life became involved in the New Age movement, running a healing and meditation centre with his partner Ingrid from a temple attached to his home. He died in 1974.

Mark Valentine is the author of several collections of short fiction and has published biographies of Arthur Machen and Sarban. He is the editor of *Wormwood*, a journal of the literature of the fantastic, supernatural, and decadent, and has previously written the introductions to editions of Walter de la Mare, Robert Louis Stevenson, L. P. Hartley, and others, and has introduced John Davidson's novel *Earl Lavender* (1895), Claude Houghton's *This Was Ivor Trent* (1935), and Oliver Onions's *The Hand of Kornelius Voyt* (1939) for Valancourt Books.

Photograph of Ronald Fraser, courtesy of Dahlia Saxby

RONALD FRASER

FLOWER PHANTOMS

With a new introduction by
MARK VALENTINE

VALANCOURT BOOKS

Flower Phantoms by Ronald Fraser
First published London: Jonathan Cape, 1926
First U.S. edition published New York: Boni & Liveright, 1926
First Valancourt Books edition 2013
Reprinted from the 1926 Boni & Liveright edition

Copyright © 1926 by Ronald Fraser, renewed 1954
Introduction © 2013 by Mark Valentine

Published by Valancourt Books, Kansas City, Missouri
Publisher & Editor: JAMES D. JENKINS
20th Century Series Editor: SIMON STERN, University of Toronto
http://www.valancourtbooks.com

ISBN 978-1-939140-10-4
Also available as an electronic book.

All Valancourt Books publications are printed on acid free paper
that meets all ANSI standards for archival quality paper.

Set in Dante MT 11/14

INTRODUCTION

RONALD FRASER's work does not earn a reference in any major study of twentieth-century English literature; neither does it appear in many studies of the fantastic in literature, though in a few he merits a bare paragraph or two. Nothing in my reading guided me to his books, only a fortunate find. In a bookshop in the cathedral city of Chichester one day, which must have been before I had reached thirty years of age, I saw a slim volume with a spine of faded green, the wan colour of a field in winter. There was a glimmer from the worn gilt of the lettering, like tired sunlight. I took up the book and was at once attracted by the title. *Flower Phantoms*. Could it possibly be a rare, lost fantasy? I opened the book to the demure pages in the good quality paper of Jonathan Cape, the publisher, and began to read.

Flower Phantoms (1926) is indeed an exquisite fantasy, about a mystic communion with the soul of an orchid in Kew Gardens, the famous botanical park in London. It is told with a fine delicacy, in a languorous, sultry prose that is apt for its setting. As a study in what the eminent scholar of the fantastic E. F. Bleiler called art deco rococoism, it is beautifully rich and sinuous. But it is also more than this. It really tells of the dawning of a young woman's independence of spirit as she finds herself through her work in horticulture, when professional women gardeners were few, and through her exploration of a more exotic mysticism than her upbringing would normally countenance. The book is also about the possibility of higher forms of consciousness, and succeeds in suggesting these without recourse to the specialist esoteric language seen in much occult fiction. It expresses rarefied states of mind with an evanescent subtlety.

These themes, of independent young women and of rarer forms of spiritual encounter, were also seen in contemporary fiction such as Stella Benson's *Living Alone* (1919) and Sylvia Townsend

Warner's *Lolly Willowes* (1926), as well as in the pagan gamines of Mary Webb's novels. They were a prevailing interest of Ronald Fraser: he returned to them frequently in subsequent novels. They are not necessarily the sort of preoccupations that might be expected from a man with Fraser's background and vocation.

Sir Arthur Ronald Fraser (1888-1974) was the fourth son of an Inverness-shire cloth merchant, who had moved to London. His father is recalled as an unimaginative man, a firm Presbyterian, hidebound in his beliefs. Fraser had a conventional education at St. Paul's School, but by his early teens was writing poetry, which was published in the *Westminster Gazette*, much to his family's amusement. At eighteen he was put to work in an insurance company, but in his spare time read at the British Museum; he was particularly interested in Buddhism. He served in the Honourable Artillery Company in the First World War, and was in the trenches by November 1914. He was seriously wounded at the battle of Beaumont-Hamel and invalided out. This left him with deep physical scars, a paralysed left arm and a claw hand, but he never let his injuries inhibit his life: he was always active and busy. He made his career in the overseas section of the Department of Trade, and in the Foreign Office, serving in Argentina and France as the Commercial Minister in the British Embassies there, and later as a Government Director of the Suez Canal, when he was resident in Egypt. His knighthood in 1949 was one of several decorations in recognition of a distinguished diplomatic career.

But he also wrote twenty-seven novels, nearly all published by Cape, between 1924 and 1961, and a few other miscellaneous books. Many of his novels are tinged with mystical fantasy. They are illumined by Fraser's deeply-held conviction that there is an order of reality superior to our familiar daily existence, and that this has the potential to show us worlds infinitely wondrous and gracious, a vision he has in common with better-known writers of the fantastic such as Arthur Machen and Algernon Blackwood. But Fraser's inspiration was largely drawn from Chinese spirituality, both Taoist and Buddhist. He never visited the Far East, but he made a deep study of its philosophy and culture.

There was a great deal of fiction inspired by Far Eastern religions in the 1920s and '30s, much of it rather breathless and winsome. Where oriental characters are not inscrutable villains, they are all-wise masters: the influence of theosophy and occultism was strong. But Fraser's work was of a different order. With only a few exceptions, his books have very English characters and settings, and he is interested in exploring how insights and concepts from China might work out if applied in the West.

Fraser's first book, *The Flying Draper* (1924) earned him comparisons to H. G. Wells, and he was in fact a great friend of Wells's oldest son, the zoologist George Philip ('Gip') Wells. His novel tells, with calm detail and subtle characterisation, how a young man in London learns, by spiritual discipline and passion, to fly of his own accord, and the confusion and hostility this provokes. It was a bold, imaginative beginning. He followed it with a book even further removed from the everyday, *Landscape With Figures* (1925). Inspired by his study of Chinese artefacts at the British Museum, this depicts the voyage of a magnate and his entourage from the South China Sea up a secret river to a Taoist paradise where three sages dwell. At once both witty and profound, the book is in one way a forerunner of James Hilton's more famous Shangri La book, *Lost Horizon* (1933). The sumptuous, strange beauty of the realm is finely and lingeringly described by Fraser.

However, these works are not in fact typical of Fraser's central body of fiction and there is much else that justifies greater interest in his writing. There are at least a handful of other novels that have a delicate distinction. The most memorable of his books is surely *Flower Phantoms*, but this was the harbinger of later work following up the themes he explored there. These works, with their celebration of the liberation of the feminine psyche, are at the heart of Fraser's vision.

In *Rose Anstey* (1930), the young hoyden of the title has a strong affinity with nature. Again, this was not an uncommon theme in its time, and the fey maiden dancing among the daisies and making friends with wild animals was a sufficient staple of interwar fiction to be frequently satirised. But Fraser is shrewder and steadier than that; his Rose is more earthbound, with a child's self-centredness and contrariety, and also its sly wisdom. She lives in an unconventional household made up of eccentrics – a worldly savant, a raffish artist and an austere hermit. Her understanding of their individual ways of life, and the development of her own way, give the book its peculiar charm and force.

His next book, *Marriage in Heaven* (1932) explores the world of a stained-glass artist, Adrian, who seeks to perfect "the charging of light with emotion" and, by analogy, the charging of life with spirit. His inspiration and distraction alike come from his wayward young lover, Linnet. Critics continued to try hard to say precisely why Fraser's work was so alluring, this time evoking "the delicate but compelling skill in conveying a sense of the undercurrents that pervade and rule our surface lives."

Again, a young woman's defiance of convention and ardent identification with the things of the spirit are proclaimed in *Miss Lucifer* (1939). Fraser had met and befriended Joan Grant, author of a highly popular series of novels based on what she believed to be her previous incarnations, beginning with *Winged Pharoah* (1937). She seems to be reflected in the title character of Miss Lucifer. Fraser himself was a firm believer in reincarnation, and in karma.

In *Maia* (1948), he conveys beautifully the pleasure in transient moments such as the experience of a shared meal, or exploring old ruins, and he captures also how the eye, or an inner eye, may see a fine significance in simple things: marrows, shadows, flowers, faces, walls and hallways. As in *Flower Phantoms*, he writes about that rare sudden sense of essence in a form, a tint, a texture, a grain. And beneath these he lightly implies an eternal truth or force at work. His characters are charming or shrewdly observed – a young married couple (both painters), an ex-soldier who studies now at the British Museum and is a sage, a brace of comfortable, hospitable widows and a practical spinster, a soothsaying charlady, two fierce and tormented young lovers, aloof French chateau-dwellers. But here he worked at greater length than the slim volume of *Flower Phantoms*: the story moves very studiedly, slowly, so needs readers who are content to linger.

Although Fraser's novels are usually intimately concerned with spirituality and the conviction of a supernal world, there is no overt insistence upon any personal deity or ultimate being, and in this he clearly differs from other writers in the field, such as C. S. Lewis and Charles Williams. Neither does Fraser make use of the concept of an active principle of evil, often the key presence in traditional ghost stories where it provides tension and opposition in the plot. Instead, the challenges facing his characters are often more human in scale and closer to everyday experience. The trials and dilemmas his characters encounter often derive from the difficulty of sustaining an identification with the numinous while locked into more mundane matters. This could become a too-solemn or programmed theme: but in *Flower Phantoms* especially, Fraser has a wonderful lightness of touch.

The critic Brian Stableford has observed acutely that a dominant theme in Fraser's work is the gulf that divides individuals who are spiritually aware from the general run of humanity who have more worldly concerns. This was perhaps the influence of his own upbringing, where his literary work and interest in Eastern religion were not understood by his family. It is certainly the case that in some of his novels, such as *The Flying Draper* and *The Fiery Gate* (1943), a well-regarded work about a grocer who is also a visionary, set during the Blitz, such seers seem doomed to find incomprehension, indifference, even scorn and resentment. But in others Fraser does imply that some sort of rapprochement between the world and the spirit is possible. This is also the inference from his own life, in which he balanced the materiality of commercial negotiations between states, the attention to the details of economic statistics and treaties, with an inner life, expressed in his books, which yielded his subtly shaded insights into spiritual experience.

In his later work he also introduced an element of the comic, with a series of four books that feature the butler Trout, a sort of interplanetary Jeeves, in space trips that are also spiritual journeys. And his final work in fiction returned more overtly to his first interest, in a group of delicate, willow-plate novels imbued with Chinese mysticism.

Late in his life, in retirement, the direction of Fraser's thought led him to what may seem his natural home in the nascent New Age movement. He and his unconventional partner Ingrid ran a healing and meditation centre from a private temple attached to their home, Swanlands, near Chinnor, Oxfordshire, and he was associated with the College of Psychic Studies and the Research Into Lost Knowledge Organisation, translating books on the symbolism of Chartres Cathedral and on an initiate of the Egyptian mysteries. It would be natural to expect that this affinity with what has proved to be an enduring new movement of the late 20th century might lead to the rediscovery of his novels, but that has not yet happened.

This is the more surprising since Fraser is a fine prose writer whose evocation of colour, shape and movement is almost tactile in its vividness. The poet Humbert Wolfe described him as "probably the most distinguished writer of English prose in the novel form at present living. He cannot do other than write beautifully." There is a chaste sensuality in Fraser's writing, and a spiritual ardour which is often the equal of the most successful passages in Machen or Blackwood, when a similarly intense mystical ecstasy is conveyed. It must surely be only a matter of time before the subtle power of his prose and the graceful conviction of his mysticism, both at their rare height in *Flower Phantoms*, receive their long-overdue recognition.

MARK VALENTINE

January 11, 2013

(With thanks to Dahlia and Michael Saxby, Ronald Fraser's daughter and son-in-law, for their recollections and their kind support of my interest in his life and books).

FLOWER PHANTOMS

§ I

K EW GARDENS were ice-bound, there was biting frost in the air, and early darkness had fallen. The world was in the death and rigor of winter, and Judy, who loved light and heat, kept indoors, when she could not be at her work in the plant-houses, like a seedling that wraps itself up close in warmth and oblivion under the ground.

They lived in a moderate and comfortable house in the lime avenue that runs from the station to the Gardens. Their father's money, which was all that survived of him, manifested itself in the house and in a moderate annuity. She lay in a window-seat under the fern-window on the first landing, over hot-water pipes – her brother, a most sensible young man, having had the house centrally heated for his own comfort. There was no light in the hall, but the mirror at the turn of the stairs dimly reflected a saffron fringe, a fern-green skirt and a pale pair of legs in the glow of an electric radiator. The eyes that gazed through a smudge of lashes seemed unusually light. Beyond the yellow head a shadowy appearance of frosted window, with a faint pattern of ferns.

She felt cold at the sight of her own legs so unkindly exposed to the draughts that circulated about the staircase. Her skirt was too short to cover her knees, so she drew up a rug, turned over, hid her face in a cushion, and tried to imagine that she was a young plant, snug in black earth over the steam-pipes of a hot-house. Her imagination was not successful at first, because there was a draught on her bare neck; but when she had managed to stop it out, and to close all other avenues by which the cold might approach her, she was able to sink into a condition beautifully comatose, a state resembling sleep, in which, among queer fragments of dreams to do with plants, she seemed once or twice about to fall into some unfamiliar night. She rescued herself from this strange experience with a start; but still she played with it; fearfully opened a door and looked out into a wintry cold and darkness of disembodiment. Even a smart pinch did not fully awake her.

The voice of her brother Hubert addressed her:

"Wake up, you cat. Why on earth do you always lie on landings? Why don't you use rooms like ordinary people?"

On her part the brother-sister spirit of dispute did not fail to respond. "Just because rooms are always full of tedious, ordinary people," she sleepily retorted.

"Well," he said, "Uncle Henry's bringing a chap to dinner who may not be so tedious. An essayist and professor of literary history. Damned clever, damned good-looking, and damned young. But he makes no money."

With that, Hubert passed on to his room. But a sort of picture of him stayed behind in the darkness of the landing; he refused to be dismissed from her thoughts; and, though she hugged the warm darkness closer, she was compelled to go over in her mind, though dimly, and as something happening in a strange exterior world, many scenes and arguments from the past. He was always a dominant figure in her imagination, with his elegance, and his brains, and his worldly wisdom. "Yes," she admitted to the shadowy figure, "you dress with distinguished taste" – if she looked up she felt she would see his elegant striped trousers in the glow of the radiator – "you are certainly handsome, with your black, pomaded hair, your long nose and your piercing, shrewd eyes. Your mind, such as it is, is ruthless; but it is a pity you have nothing to exercise your brains on save the notion of financial success. You are attractive – I perceive it, and I admit it – to women. But two things you are mortally afraid of – poverty . . . and me!"

The figure of her brother smiled back at her jibes with the air of one who retains his self-confidence. That, she remembered, was how he had always met her – as when she remarked that all he had learned at school was enough arithmetic to calculate the sum invested in his mother's annuity. "Really," she said to the smiling shadow, "you never needed school. From the first you saw things as they are."

How she had scoffed at his lack of imagination when he went into insurance! But how, at the same time, he had flourished in that unseen city world she heard of out there in the cold!

He grew amazingly, she remembered, and lost in a few days all traces of the illusions of youth. At eighteen and one month he understood investment, and his knowledge, he had told her, confirmed an unfavorable opinion, formed some years earlier, of his father's capacity. As regards his attitude towards their mother, she felt, secretly, and hiding her face in the cushions, able to approve him. Their mother was a weak, plump woman with asthma; she had no feeling for business and no brains (though there were men of science in her family and one of them, Uncle Henry, was in charge of Kew Gardens); so at eighteen and a half he interviewed her lawyer, and it was not long before that gentleman was ready to admit so shrewd, so informed, so businesslike a youth to the management of her affairs. At nineteen the house was organized to his liking; he ruled his mother, and as in effect he controlled the income, apart from what she earned by scientific journalism, was able to frustrate her own expensive desires. At twenty-one he had a handsome coupé and was a member of several night clubs. At twenty-five he had nearly completed the extensive foundations of what would presently be a considerable business. He argued that it was unnecessary to move from the moderate house in the lime avenue; soon enough his sister would marry and his mother would die, and there was no reason why he should give them more than they had already.

"But let nobody think that I dislike you," she said, suddenly realizing that any one who overheard what was going on in her mind would have gathered that she thought unkindly of her brother. "It is only that you're a fool for thinking you see things as they are."

How are things? She asked herself that question, and as the difficulty of answering it became more and more apparent the figure of Hubert faded out of her reverie. Soon, too, she became impa-

tient of the new argument, and let her mind sleep. Now she was in
silence and warmth, wrapped up and hidden once more like a seed
in the blackness of earth, with no knowledge of anything outside,
conscious only of tiny internal changes, nor desiring the unknown
splendor of summer suns.

§ II

THE Gardens were under snow when she allowed herself to
become party to an engagement with the young man whom
Uncle Henry brought to dinner.

It was a sudden, an unpremeditated consent. They were walking in the Arboretum, she in the corduroy jacket and breeches of a
student gardener, plowing her way through the snow with a green
stalk in her mouth like a golden stable-boy. She pleased herself
with the fancy that the gray clouds were showering down lilies-of-
the-valley, and that she was flinging the faintly-scented missiles at
Roland.

Roland was big, brown and scholarly, with a wave of dark
umber hair; and very distinguished, very picturesque he looked
in the white woods; and very apt were his quotations from the
world's literature, very distinguished, occasionally, his own original phrases. He was a hard and accurate shot with a snowball, and
perhaps an unexpected pleasure that she experienced in the swift-
ness of his attack and the completeness of her defeat predisposed
her to submission in another respect.

It was a physical contest, and she lost. In all other contests she
had won. And now, in the glow of the moment, she let him kiss her
– this after weeks of ardor on his part and ironical observation on
hers. As they kissed she looked over his shoulder, and there across
the white lawns she saw those steamy plant-houses whose warmth
and secret life she so loved. Remembered sensations abated the
sensation of the kiss. He took her into the hidden bamboo garden, among shivering plants, and there repeated his kisses. She was
not so confident now, and soon she began to shrink, for he was so

rough, so boreal, and she felt like a tender shoot that has come up in the snow and would have done better to stay underground.

Her shrinking distressed him, but he had not the skill to restore her to willingness, or the wit to leave her alone. He even tried, when they had left that icy garden, to snowball her again into submission. This, she perceived, was clumsy, and his inability to treat her in such a way as to reawaken impulse annoyed her.

They began to walk homeward, along a deep winter-shadowy path in noiseless snow, between rhododendron bushes that bore round, large and chilly flowers. He wooed her with compliments, and gave up snowballs for phrases.

"You look like some golden boy," he said. "Your hair" – these words had given him some pains to assemble – "is cut in such a way that it seems to be a cap of gold, or helmet of saffron fire. Your eyes are a pale and mysterious gray, like a snowing sky, yet they have specks of a strong pigment, sky-blue and topaz; and you have surprising dark fringes, so that the eyes stare out under the shining hat like those of a princely, dreaming, mischievous, and cynical page in some wintry and Russian court."

She found it interesting to be described, and slipped her hand through his arm. Thus encouraged he renewed the attack.

"You move in this white world like a torch."

She did not think that good, and was silent.

"You are a yellow daffodil blooming in the snow."

There was a chilly reminder there with her own sensations in the bamboo garden, and she shivered.

"A firefly among snowdrops," he continued. He was looking at her tenderly, and she made use of her favorite weapon.

"And you are a polar bear," was her answer. From the first she had given his compliments this sort of arctic reception, and replied to him with blizzards, to the astonishment of his soul. But this time he was exasperated.

"You are an annoying little devil!" he cried. "If I were a polar bear I'm damned if I wouldn't hug you till you scrunched!"

"I think I should like that," she replied, soberly examining the possibilities of such a situation.

He should not have then tried to kiss her.

"Damn it!" he protested. "I don't know what to make of you. You don't seem to mean what you say. You don't seem to know your mind!"

"I don't," she said. "It would be most interesting to find out what one meant, and what one wanted, and what one was really like inside. I'm sure one contains the most queer possibilities. And there are fires laid, if any one could light them."

He was angry. "Psychological discussions are for the classroom."

She made no rejoinder. They were passing the greenhouses.

§ III

AFTER a few minutes of walking in a constrained silence, they found themselves outside the moderate and comfortable house in the lime avenue. It nestled under a weight of snow. There were red berries in the front garden, ferns in the window, and solid silver, reflecting a glowing fire, on the sideboard.

"Am I to leave you?" he coldly asked.

She glanced at him, standing there in the cloud of his own breath. It did not seem desirable that the matter should be decided there and then.

"Of course you are not to leave me. You are to come in and have tea."

Shrugging, he consented.

"It is odd," she reflected, as he took off his great shaggy overcoat, "how active a relationship between two people is; how rapidly ties are formed; how soon you find yourself more or less committed."

The elegant Hubert was at home. "Hullo!" he said, looking at their faces, "what have you two been up to?"

"Nothing," they both replied at once.

"Don't tell me there's anything on. Don't say there's any rot about an engagement." Hubert brutally knew the world and was frank.

Did Roland, who looked so foolish, feel the same absurd excitement that she did on finding herself thus interestingly linked with him?

She pulled her brother's pomaded hair. "Whatever we've been doing, it's no business of yours, my child."

He stared at her. "I perceive that the worst is about to happen." He addressed Roland. "As my sister's guardian . . ."

"You're nothing of the kind!" she flamed.

"As my sister's moral guardian," he continued, "I require you, before you go on making love to her, and possibly, if you are a man of experience, making her fond of you, to state, apart from other matters on which I must make inquiry, the extent of your income."

Roland, no man of the world, was helpless. "Some four or five hundred a year," he lamely replied.

Hubert threw up his hands. "Good God! I always thought you were mad, Judy. . . ."

"But," Roland stammered, "but we are not engaged. . . ."

"And you will not be," replied Hubert.

Anything that Hubert denied her Judy must have. "Yes, we shall!" she burst out.

Then all at once she felt hopelessly compromised.

§ IV

THE days were lengthening; the frost had given way to mud and warm rain. Scented rain it seemed to Judy, and sometimes she saw May in the February horizon. Here and there shoots were pushing up through the sticky mold, little spears that pierced into her heart and woke intolerable longings for the spring and the time of flowers.

She and Roland were eating their lunch in a shop with large windows near the station. Hubert happened to be at home, and although, with frank prophecies of disaster, he had withdrawn his opposition to her published will in regard to Roland, she preferred, sometimes, not to submit her private mind to his brutal inquisition.

"In February," she observed, "it rains violets. The roofs of houses are wet with them and there are pools of them lying among the trees."

"That is true," said Roland, with an ardent glance. She did not return it. Roland was ardent in season and out, and she disliked it. Why could he not reply to her thought with something relevant and poetic?

The waitress brought their luncheon – eggs and coffee for her, the charred ruins of a steak pie for him. He must choose something masculine like steak. He produced on her always an effect of masculinity – of tweed, tobacco and clumsy thought.

"Why did the waitress smile at us so kindly?" she inquired.

"Because we are lovers. And not unpresentable," he modestly added.

It was the case. Everybody smiled on them. As a scientific student, one who must not overlook any fact, she had to admit that she herself was an object of rare loveliness. People had often told her so; and there she was, anyway, in the huge mirror, so golden and delicate that it surprised her. She stared at her own mysterious light gray eyes. As to Roland, she had to admit a distinguished appearance. There was a refined sort of scholarly beauty hiding in the strong lines of his brown, handsome face. It was a beauty that might become spiritual. There was in his nature – she had seen it in flashes – a light that if it woke might illuminate his lovemaking. Certainly they were a handsome couple, and it was true that people smiled on them. Sometimes it was not unexciting to be smiled on as if one were a bride. Sometimes their smiles were gaolers.

She would not talk. She felt reflective and spiritual and full of delicate sensations. The second egg, as she thoughtfully tapped it, seemed too gross a food for the ethereal condition of her body. She left it, and amused herself with gazing through the plate-glass windows. The light in the sky fascinated her and she fell into a queer state of mind.

The rain had stopped, the crocus-clouds were drifting out of the sky, there was a warmth of the sun and faint stirring of the earth.

"You are forgetting your egg." It was Roland's voice and she met his eyes studying her.

"Oh!" she exclaimed. "It's the glass. I mean, I felt the light on me and I was thinking what it would be like to be a plant in a greenhouse."

"What nonsense!" He spoke roughly, but there was anxiety in his face. "Your pale, pale eyes looked so queer," he added.

If he could but have followed her into the world of her imagination! But he only sat there consuming steak and kidney pie like a porter. She did not understand him. For Roland reality seemed to be verbal; but his range of perceptions was limited, and that was perhaps why his juggling with words was unsuccessful. He was literary, and life did not emerge from his synthetic experiments. And into his flimsy world of phrases there rushed gross appetites, untranslated. He had no delicacies of his own: they were all verbal and vanished before the onrush of desire. Appetite! Bad enough in the matter of food, but in the matter of love . . . she shrank from him. Yet she knew this was not quite fair. She knew that her nerves made rather a bogy of his desires. And she knew that there was in herself, deep enough down at present, a person who would not shrink.

She defended her dream. "Why shouldn't one know what it's like to be a plant?"

"Because plants are entirely different."

"Your knowledge, except where classical literature is concerned, is defective," she pointed out. "We know now that the plant and the animal are not so different. They breathe, there is circulation of fluid by pumping, pulsatory movement from cell to cell, and similar nervous mechanism. All life is the same. A daffodil and I are similar creatures in dissimilar circumstances. . . ."

"You are right," he interrupted. "You are a daffodil, a yellow daffodil."

She frowned. "If you can't talk reasonably on a scientific subject I will go back to work." She gave him no opportunity to protest, but left the table and demanded her bill. She had seen the plant-houses in a vision and her soul longed for them – for the heat, the living silence, the secret activity and thinking of plants. For there were presences among the plants, unseen and noiseless forms, green spirits mimicking the appearance of leaf or stalk. "I believe," she thought, trying to see herself, "that I am more poetical than scientific. But there are points of contact between these two types of mind."

§ V

FROM her lair under the fern-window she heard Roland and Hubert discussing her in the parlor. They had left the door open, and it seemed to her that it might be in everybody's best interests for her to overhear. That was a leaf from her brother's book, she reflected, and cocked a snook in the direction of the elegant figure that would be sitting in a chair in the sunny window – too self-confident to have to stand in an argument – while Roland restlessly fingered the curios that her father had collected in his travels.

It was the first day of summer time. She had found the unaccustomed length of the afternoon somewhat inconsonant with the virginal and shrinking beauty of early April. It had seemed a little unearthly and produced some disharmony in her which Roland had not the skill to deal with.

"Where is she?" asked Hubert. "Do you want me to say something to her?"

"She is sitting on the landing under her 'fern-window.' I left her there, I distrust that window. It gives her queer feelings, evidently, for her eyes go strange when she gazes at it."

"I shall have it taken away and a window of ordinary glass put in its place," said Hubert with decision. "I cannot imagine, in any case, why anybody should choose to have a window of glass you can't see through with patterns of ferns all over it. Windows are meant to see through, and to let light in."

"It does let light in," she heard Roland reply. "It seems to gather and intensify and whiten the light. Sometimes in the afternoon, she says, it's like sitting under a Niagara of light with trees flaming down in it."

"Sensible people do not sit on landings gazing at ferns in a window. They sit in rooms. That is what rooms are for. Or if it is summer, in gardens. That is what gardens are for."

"Well," Roland seemed to agree, "I don't like it when she looks at the light for a quarter of an hour at a time till her eyes – those pale, unrelenting eyes – get so full of it that she doesn't notice me."

"I gather she has offended you."

"No. Not that." He impatiently brushed the hair from his brow – she knew his gesture: "I have offended myself. I do not succeed with her. She is so mocking, critical, and keen-minded. I can't – do you know what I mean? – I can't get the upper hand. I mean, she is not in love with me. Not abandonedly, not of necessity, and with that desperation, that addition of glorious madness we read about. She loves me, I fear, with discernment, though on occasion with ardor, I must admit. I must admit that, though I do not understand it. She has been eager, I must tell you, on occasion, and . . . how shall I put it? . . . experimental – within what is delicate, of course. But each time I seem to disappoint her."

She smiled. And then almost she wept. She had relied on his knowing how to summon up the resources of love that were hidden in her nature, and direct them on himself. But he had proved so clumsy.

"You cannot be very adroit, I suppose." Hubert spoke with a certain shade of contempt. "Instinct is lacking and you have not become expert by practice."

There was a sound of defeat in Roland's answer. "I do not really know why she has said she'll marry me."

"No doubt because you are handsome, incapable of business and hard up. Or really, I suppose, because of some unreasonable correspondence in your respective chemistries. Or again, as electrical engineers say, you are in resonance. It is absurd, but it is a fact, and we cannot disregard it."

"But I fear it is not a fact. The correspondence is not quite perfect, and the resonance is not more than almost complete. It is that infinitesimal disharmony that is so damnably baffling."

"Well, I must say I don't understand it. Any man with an average amount of brains and good looks can make any woman in love with him, if he cares to take the trouble."

"Is that your experience?" asked Roland enviously.

"My experience," replied Hubert, giving the subject more searching attention, "is that it is easy to give movement and direction to a woman's wishes, to become the object of her secret instincts, and thus, always prudently, to enlist her will on the side of your amusement."

"What cheek!" she commented. "And what a lie!"

"But I think you have more than the average you mention," said Roland's voice. "Certain advantages – good looks, though by themselves they are nothing: a certain – what would one say? – distinction is almost the word – a grace, a charm, a magnetism, that is instantly effective with women and without it one does not interest them, except with great difficulty. Still, in this case, you have not dominated."

"Ass! She is my sister."

But this aspect of the question had ceased to interest Roland. Glancing, perhaps, through the window he had seen the delicate April sky, and made sensitive by love experienced a rush of emotion not referable to classic sources.

"She is so lovely!" he cried. "When I die I shall never have found her description. She is an experience that has never been realized in language, Hubert. She is not Cleopatra, Nicolette, or Beatrice, though she has some quality of each, as passionateness, naïveté, and power of soul. She is a flower. Lily! Daffodil! If only I might be given one flash of vision, one swift phrase of searching beauty, one spear-pointed word to use with her – she would be my victim!" There was a pause, during which he evidently fell from his lyric height. "I must sound like a fool. But you know how maddening her beauty is – her beauty like a yellow radiance with that subtle remorseless brain thinking secretly in the midst of it." His feelings surged again. "You know how exquisite, how fragrant, how . . ."

Hubert interrupted. "As I said before," he remarked, "she is my sister."

§ VI

THEY sat together one afternoon in the window-seat on the landing, in the April radiance of the fern-window, he dark and frowning with his desire for her, she slender, golden, young. She wore a white blouse and over it her jacket of brown corduroy, breeches of the same and puttees.

Now he tilted back the small head and spoke almost on her mouth.

"You are a golden lily."

She stared past him at the light of the window.

"Your feet and your hands are snowdrops," he continued. "You have daffodil-yellow hair." She let her lashes begin to droop mockingly, but he went on. "Your flesh is narcissus-stuff."

Her eyes dwelt on him for a minute and the grasp of his hands tightened. "But my lips and eyes," she pointed out, "you have not mentioned them."

"I'm coming to those," he said grimly. "Your lips are poppies and breathe the opium of some paradise. Your eyes . . ."

"One would say I was really an extremely hybrid flower," she interrupted.

"And your eyes," he went on with desperation, "your eyes are the pale petals of the anemone. It is like staring into the golden eye of narcissus. There is something that looks out of a flower's eye, but one cannot say where or what."

"I am now catalogued," she replied, "but my description has not moved me. You must try again."

He searched in her eyes, and she kept them still and blind as deep water. Presently he gave out the result of a prolonged inspection. "The iris is light cloud-gray. Or blue? Topaz? Impossible

to decide. Mostly a bluish-gray, but there are certainly streaks or
spots of a fiery topaz. The pupil is a black well. One can see no
bottom." His face impended. "It is mechanical. There are little
sudden contractions and expansions. The eye when you look into
it is made of very curious stuff." His voice carried a note, one
would have said, of fear – the fear of a romantic when the light
fades for a moment off his illusion. "My God! Judy, the human
eye is a very terrifying thing. It's so inhuman. There's no soul in
it. It's a machine. A lot of cloudy, spongy, extremely queer stuff,
with a sinister black hole. It's expressionless, when you look close.
Laughter, kindness, everything that makes people human, seems
to disappear. What a strange and terrible thing mind must be; how
curious, how frightening, those movements in a queer kind of
matter that one calls thought. I can't stand it!" He stood away from
her, to recapture the humanness of her eyes, but still they seemed
so light, so changeless, so impersonal. "For heaven's sake, what is
going on behind your eyes!" he exclaimed. "Can't you stop staring
at the window!"

She smiled, under her cap of fire, to break the spell of fear in
which, as she saw, he had become bound. "I was thinking of a
forest of waving ferns, inhabited only by large silken cats."

"Oh, you and your ferns! Are you plant-mad, Judy?"

"It is possible," she replied. "When I get among them . . . something happens. When I am in that universe bounded by tinted
glass, in an ether magical with light, warmth, my critical wits leave
me. I become an irrealist, like you, and live in a self-created world.
There's a glow, a smell of heat and water, of mold, of the green
bodies of flowers. I see a sort of order, a reality, in the relations of
flower and leaf and viridescent stem; or, I should say, behind them:
it is suggested. And sometimes there is a strange thing happens –
as if spirits I have known, spirits of people who are dead, clung in
the flowers and were beckoning me." She pondered deeply, striving for means of expression adequate to her experiences – then
gave it up. "But oh! I don't know. . . ." And she reflected that he
would not have understood her: she had been where he was not
delicate-minded enough to follow.

The sadness that she felt must have shown in her face, for he took and kissed her. "My golden lily! I could eat you."

"Ah! Now you are talking sense!"

She saw his swift hope, when he perceived that he had succeeded in interesting her senses, and it seemed maladroit of him, greedy. She fled into her armor of criticism. "But you must understand, my Roland, it is no good using that language about flowers with me. I live with them. I know them. I know the world of the plants, their thoughts, their feelings, and I have intimations of strange experiences among them. No image, therefore, that you could fetch from the furthest of your literary excursions would ever cope with the real flower, or with the experience, or with any experience . . ." she began to expand her thesis.

"I disagree," he said, professionally wounded. "The great poets can make effects with words that nature could never hope to equal."

"Well," she admitted, "it is true that what you said then about eating me was effective. It makes me realize the depth of your love. Sometimes I bite the hearts out of roses. I am a sadist, with flowers."

"You are lovely, cruel, and irrefutable as life itself. Ah! There is a new change in the sunset-irradiated iris-cloud. Have I used some expression that amuses you?"

"Irrefutable," she said. "You have stirred your public with the word 'irrefutable.'" But she held him at arm's length. "Will life always be irrefutable, I wonder? There must come a time, I suppose, when life will become senile, and fail to effect its will. Or some formidable change in the condition of the planet . . ."

"The words sound most beautiful on your boyish mouth," he interjected.

". . . some change," she continued, "which even life, tough as it is, can't stand. Or a dissolution of matter, so that there is nothing which can exhibit the characteristics. It will be sad for scientists, when the subject of research disappears under their own vanishing hands."

"And what will there be left?" he asked, depressed, doubtless, by her detachment.

"The original nothing, I presume. Whatever that may be. A chance for some one to invent another kind of reality."

"This is an education for me," he responded, not without resentment. "I am improved by your conversation. I didn't really hope that you would say love would be left. Still, it is an achievement to have awakened these reflections. You express them well. Myself, I am not expressive, as you so often and so rightly say, unless I have access to dictionaries and books of reference. But are you not just a little sad" – he spoke sardonically – "that on the occasion to which you refer there will no longer be any means for the contact of lips in love; not even memories to remember it?"

"You are getting angry with me," she said, suddenly lifting her small, golden head. "I like it."

The fire was dying out of the fern-window and they were in the shadows of dusk. It came to her suddenly that she was desirous of kisses. He drew her close. She became very still, and let her restless mind drowse.

"Why have you said that perhaps you'll marry me?" he presently asked, bewildered, no doubt, by her changes of mood.

"Because I love you," she whispered, "at moments, unreasonably."

"Why do you love me," he pressed, "at moments, unreasonably?"

She replied to his question with a shyness that stroked from his nerves the last anguish of pleasure (there was a sting, too, in what she said): "In this matter of kissing me, at any rate, you are sometimes not unconvincing."

Now she let her nerves drown under the torrent of his kisses. It was vehement enough to overwhelm any resistances or protests of expiring criticism.

§ VII

A FEW days after, in the morning, Roland came seeking Judy throughout the plant-houses in Kew Gardens. She had forbidden him to do it; but he explained that he desired to see her at

work; to know what it was about those flowers and ferns that, as
he may have surmised, made her a little mad; to surprise her, if he
might, in the supposed condition, observe her, and try to understand. Flowers were all very well. He knew about them, of course,
through the images in literature. Without doubt he was aware that
they existed, as the occasion of numerous fancies and thoughts to
do with grace, purity, transience and the like. But she believed that
his heart never missed a beat at the sudden advance of a troop of
daffodils in a meadow; an azalea blowing like flame did not bewil-
der him with irrational suggestions, that one distrusted, of a presence hidden in the wind, of words spoken soundlessly about one;
he did not feel the teeming of an unperceived order of existence,
an inexpressible reality.

"I saw you," he told her presently, "through the glass of the
cactus house as through water, and you looked like a tow-headed
nymph in some African river full of dim, prickly weeds." The door
was not locked and he had stolen in, closing the door quietly, with
the idea of watching her at work. While he stood with his hand on
the door-handle, she had turned half round and seemed to stare
into the tangle of cactuses and euphorbias; it might have been the
very tiny click of the latch that disturbed her. Then she bent her
small, shining head over the plant on which she was operating, and
stood there capably with her back to him, her legs straddled, her
elbows busily moving, and sometimes she cleaned a knife on the
seat of her breeches.

After a few minutes of stillness, it seems, he felt he should be
compelled to speak. The silence was broken, and the dry heat
relieved, only by an intolerable drip of water from a tap somewhere. The sun burned in the glass roof as in the fierce and scorch-
ing sky of the Sahara. In the end he broke the tension involuntarily,
found quite unexpectedly that he had loudly turned the knob of
the door and was shuffling his feet.

"I wanted to observe you," he apologized, at the stare of her
eyes, "and you were so charming that I began to desire you."

"The state is not favorable to observation," she said shortly. "I
could never work if I felt like that."

"Your behavior, though, when you found that some one was present, was not a little odd," he contested; "for one so self-possessed and so icy-proof against poor desiring devils like me you seemed a trifle confused. Why did you look so anxiously into the tangle of plants, as if to reassure yourself that some one was safely hidden?" He must have seen plainly, and obviously it was baffling, that nobody was hidden; it was quite clear that he and she were alone in the hothouse – alone, but for the brooding plants, and the prickly silence. But for him there was no voice in the silence; there were no eyes among the plants. The thought that he might come near to her state of mind perished.

"Why have you come when I told you not to?" she demanded, still in a little confusion.

"I'm sorry," he apologized. "I wanted to see you at work . . . what it is that interests you so much."

Ordinarily she would have put his question off with some irrelevant answer. To-day, she was discomposed enough to reply, speaking low, as if she could be overheard: "It is necessary that I should know the life of plants." Perhaps she still had some hope that he would understand her.

"Oh, life!" he interjected. "Nasty raw stuff!"

At that she recovered. She perceived that for him reality was merely verbal; the situation could be saved by the manipulation of words. She glanced at him, leant against the trays and crossed one leg over the other. "You do not like your life crude. Even your kisses," she mocked, "are a trifle literary. Exquisite, but chosen and just. They smack of the midnight oil. I admit it. No . . . not now." She prevented him.

"I don't know why . . . the image is possibly far-fetched . . . but for the moment your eyelids remind me of the petals of pansies."

"I was up late last night," she answered.

He stood away from her and examined her face. "Your eyes," he said, "are ringed with a faint, purplish darkness as of imagined pansy petals. The image is not far-fetched," he concluded. "It is true."

"But still, it is an image. More flowers!" She groaned.

"There is no flower here that can equal . . . Oh, hell! I was beginning again. But really it is true, what I was going to say, that there is
no flower in all these gardens that can equal the texture and sweetness of your skin."

"Oh," she said, "I could show you something in the orchid
house . . ."

She broke off. The flower she spoke of was the subject of
certain intimate thoughts. The beauty and the strength of that
orchid were mysteriously more efficient with her senses than the
beauty and strength of Roland.

"I agree," she recovered, "that I am perhaps unequaled in this
particular neighborhood. Most of these plants are extremely ugly
and horrible."

These words were spoken with emphasis, as if meant for ears.

He glanced at the cactuses, the huge many-armed euphorbias.

"Those spiky things look as if their flesh would be unpleasant,"
he observed.

"Extremely loathsome."

"Their habits distasteful."

"Excessively revolting."

"And their life, that raw stuff we were speaking of, unpleasing,
like the life of butchers and some kinds of old men."

"You have said it," she concluded. "But they are not all like that.
The bodies of most plants are pleasant, and some are very delicate
and aromatic. You are not, of course, to think that I am trying to
isolate the life of plants as if it were a juice. It has now been posi-
tively shown by physicists and chemists that there is really no such
thing as life. What I seek is to know their desires. . . ."

"Desires? How can plants have desires?"

"They have needs," she pointed out; "therefore probably
desires."

"But they have no consciousness to be aware of themselves as
possessing desires."

"How do you know? What is consciousness? Anyway, that is
what I am after, to know their queer civilization, what they have
built up from their raw life; and, as fundamental, what it is in them

that is in us too. I mean, what there is of common origin and, if you understand me, common experience."

"I see." But he was not inspired. He thought. "As to common origin, it is a question for scientists to agree upon, and inform us with Roman-pontifical authority what has been decided. It does not interest me. But as to what they have built up out of their raw life, how they have contrived to protect themselves against life, it is a question that interests a scholar, for it has its parallel in the humanities." He spoke smilingly, as one who pretends something for a child's amusement. "You will agree with me that life in itself, the mere passage of the mind and senses through the cold medium of time, is unpleasant, really very painful. We all take infinite pains to protect ourselves against it, and so, possibly, do your plants. Those who have no distraction for the nervous and muscular system, those who have nothing to do, sleep, if they can, and if they can't go mad. The pleasures of thought, contemplation itself, are also a protection against life. The study of literature is the noblest distraction, and teaches us how noble men have distracted themselves in the past."

"That may be so," she answered, gazing with evident boredom into the well of truth, "but it is experiences that distract me, not descriptions."

"You like your senses. The simple truth is that your senses are the chief part of you: you think with them. They are very delicate, I know. Very delicate and shy. I know it too well!"

She bit her lip, thinking. She knew that she was in danger of her senses – but could it be merely the senses that sent those curious intimations and threatened to be convincing about things that a critical and sarcastic brain really could not approve? Presently, from her seeming abstraction, came a teasing reply with spines on it, like the cactuses.

"Your simple truth might do for a character in a novel, where all truth ought to be simple. But you have not completely described me. No doubt I am not living to you, but only a character, a figment, an assemblage of images."

He did not fail to demonstrate his opinion on this point, and she did not shrink, this time. And why, at this moment, had she provoked him? "Am I living to you?" he asked.

"Undoubtedly," she said, "when you kiss me. You express yourself unmistakably, in kisses. Your style is vigorous and exact. But how could one know that anybody was living and real, except through the senses?" She was more interested in her thoughts, really, than in his love. "If one felt that there was some one or something that one could not see, hear, or feel, one could not let oneself be convinced. Although no doubt there are activities that we cannot perceive with the senses we have. If one could dream oneself down out of human life into the state of undifferentiated existence, might not one re-emerge in some other direction, as a plant, for example? At any rate one might see into the consciousness of plants. But that is just a theory, and one cannot consent to a theory, can one? They are always too neat to be true, aren't they?" He kept a morose silence. "Aren't they?" she plagued.

The relevance of his answer was not at once clear. "I shall never make you love me."

A lover is not wise to permit himself this admission. But he looked so unhappy that at the least she felt some slight compunction.

"I do not see the point," she observed, not without solicitude.

"I sometimes fear that you may turn out to be that uncomfortable thing, an artist. . . ."

"I wonder." It was true that she was always trying to describe to herself her impressions of the plants, and always drawing plants or the parts of plants. These drawings, in particular, constantly dissatisfied her. They lacked something that looked out from the real flowers.

"It is certain," he went on, "that you have experienced more than I. A man should precede a woman in experience, if she is to love him. What hope can I have, then?"

In view of his sadness, she put up her chin. "You are brown and beautiful, and you smell of tweed," she pointed out. Then, though she protested "My work," he sat down on the scorched stone and lifted her on to his knees. She shivered when the spikes of a cactus pricked her shoulder.

She suffered him, now, to search all her face and consider the slender body that he held in his arms. She permitted him to push aside the corduroy jacket, and the blouse, and kiss the hollow in her shoulder.

Presently she lifted her face.

"It would be exquisite to be hugged by a cactus, all prickly and hurting; to bleed to death in a delicious, agonizing embrace."

"What a funny thing to say." Again he hopelessly searched her eyes – the eyes of a silken cat – that were fixed on the tinted and exotic splendors of sunlight diffused in a glass sky. Then suddenly she stiffened her body, and shifted her gaze to the tangle where the huge, many-armed euphorbia grew. She sat up, pulled the corduroy jacket swiftly over her bosom and drew a little comb from her breeches pocket and arranged her hair – how it seemed to stream under the comb like waves under a glowing sun!

"There's nobody," he remonstrated.

"No, but really, I thought . . . I thought some one spoke!"

He looked at her in extreme bewilderment.

§ VIII

NEXT day Judy issued the most stringent instructions that she was not to be disturbed at her work by Roland. But with the certainty of solitude she found herself reluctant to enter that plant-house where her work lay. The experience that she guessed (against the arguments of her brain) awaited her was one that she feared. It was so irrational; or rather, rational in accordance with a so far-fetched reasoning. It would never be a thing to talk about, for one could not risk the suspicion of being the subject of hallucinations.

She stopped, on her way to the greenhouse, and said good-morning to three gardeners who were planting hyacinths in a bed. One was old, the second middle-aged, the third young.

"A lovely morning," she proffered.

"Yes, miss," said the old one, and the young one stared at her sulkily. But she had noted that her appearance often made youths sulky.

"Have you been here a very long time?" she asked the oldest gardener.

"Fifty years, miss."

"Then you have a very long experience of plants. They are curious things, are they not?"

"Yes, miss."

"There are plants that move about, as you know."

"Yes, miss."

"Have you yourself ever had any curious experience of a plant?"

"No, miss."

Discouraging. At the brink of a profound experience one instinctively looks round for human company. But the young gardener seemed eager to help.

"I've 'eard of queer things since I took up with these 'ere 'ot'ouse plants," he said. He was young and ready to stretch a point, if it should win him favor.

"I've 'eard of a plant wot spoke," said the middle-aged one gruffly. "It repeated itself. It was a onion." Thus he intimated his opinion of mysteries.

She tolerated his joke. "A cinerary protest," she remarked, and passed on frowning.

The three, she knew (she was always vividly aware of herself), were looking at her saffron-headed figure as it went down the path with its boyish attire and its womanish glide. She imagined their observations. The angry, middle-aged one would use language in which an apparently incontinent aunt was somehow involved with the future of his eyes; the old man would reserve his opinion, or come out unexpectedly on her side and say that he doubted there was no harm in it; and the young one, purified by her loveliness, would make it known that if the middle-aged one had any more to say, he himself, on behalf of the good and the beautiful, would be ready to knock his head (described with an adjective that she felt was inappropriate as applied to heads) off his similarly described neck. Then she came abreast of two old ladies on a seat, and laughed to think of their horror could they have heard the language then passing in the sleek head of that demure, gliding girl.

§ IX

SHE stopped at the door of the plant-house and peered in. Then, setting her teeth in her lower lip, she turned the knob and entered the illimitable and mysterious universe in which her imagination was a flying angel. There was no wind in there – nothing but green-golden, rose-golden, brown-golden light in a sky of glass, a smell of heat and water and the bodies of plants, and a reverberation throughout the teeming plant silence. She held on a moment before letting the door quite close. She wanted to retain direct contact with the more usual world, just as, in her imagination, she always wanted to keep open the road back to common sense. She was nervous. She passed a half-hour in somewhat strained attention to work – she was engaged on a research into the curious relationships between the Western cactuses and the tropical Eastern euphorbias – and all the time it seemed as if somebody was creeping behind, twitching at her blouse (in the hot-houses she always pulled off her jacket) and stroking her hair. But hard as she might pretend to be occupied, and swiftly as she might turn her head, nothing was to be detected.

Then, as nothing happened (and what could happen, idiot? her brain contemptuously demanded), she began to think of Roland. How foolish it is, her thoughts ran, to be apprehensive of danger because one is alone. For nothing that can happen to one is really terrifying, taking a long view. Not even, say, the loss of one's loveliness? Not even that, taking a long, a very long view. If Roland were here, he would be kissing me, between whiles; as often as possible, in fact. There is really, she pointed out to herself, developing the thought so as to occupy her mind, no limit to the length of a kiss; except, for those who have not true passion, the craving for food; no limit, for an artist can always breathe through the nose. It was her custom to ruminate in this manner, even when her senses were occupied. Often, when she was suffering his kisses, she would inspect her reactions to the single blurred eye that met her own (blurred also, she supposed); or she would admit to herself that the kiss was not satisfying, and coolly plan some voluptuous movement of her lips, or other device, to madden her friend with advantage to herself. But such exercises on her part would be unthought of if she were completely in love: these were physical fillips for a spirit that refused to go full gallop; spurs that one would not ask for, or feel, in the authentic passion.

She dismissed these thoughts with a shake of her daffodil head, and began a new search for mental occupation. She pondered, dimly, the adaptations of the cacti to the stimulus of light. Would they vary in some perhaps not measurable way when the light that came down through the golden and glassy medium of that universe was so magical? The stems of some phyllo-cacti before her, grown in the dark, were mere rods, instead of resembling fleshy leaves like the stems of those grown in the light. She seemed to be able to watch the photosynthetic organs of the atrophied cacti drinking in light, as a thirsty man drinks water. And the properly nourished ones were at it, too, steadily and complacently, with no glances of solicitude for their starving fellows. After all, there's plenty of their sort of food, she reflected; no need, therefore, for anybody to be greedy. She remembered, of course, that in less generous surroundings they might have struggled ruthlessly for light, for existence. If "struggle" is not a question-begging word – she made a note of that for further thought. But here there was no need for anybody to starve – unless we presumably unseen gods of this upper world order otherwise. Is it upper? She answered herself, and question proceeded from answer, answer followed question, until she was quite translated into a world of plants that ate and communicated like men. If they could only come part of the way to meet her, as she had gone to meet them. If they would appear to her in a shape somewhat resembling the shape of men, so that one could speak of face, or eyes. She pretended, like a child, that they could. If they would dress their plant-thoughts in a kind of human speech, so that one could have a sort of conversation. But not in this house. One would not want to converse with these unpleasant plants. The thought spoilt the strange pleasure that she was experiencing. The Euphorbia, for instance, would have somewhat the likeness of one of those wrinkled, tightly packed old gentlemen that are seen on a fine spring afternoon: ghoulish and debauched specters of a lustful youth, stained corpses, infecting the sunshine, raised from the dead by miracle-working April.

She suffered as if such a creature were actually trying to ingratiate her; just as if she were really under his horrible inspection she turned this way and that, and every way some part of her, she felt, gave him pleasure.

Was there actually a voice, repeating her sentence of yesterday? "'It would be exquisite to be hugged by a cactus, all prickly and hurting; to bleed to death in a delicious, agonizing embrace!' Thank you, my dear, thank you. Ah, how it warmed my old nerves to hear that, and set them tingling."

She realized that she had herself created this curious experience, but she hurried from the plant-house. For one who desired to come to some intimate knowledge of plants, it was a disappointing introduction.

§ X

In the fern-window that evening the still head that lay in the refuge of Roland's breast was considering many things. She was engaged in deciding the future. He, she knew well, was distressed by her silence, by the impersonal stare of the tiny black holes in the midst of her cloud-gray irises; he knew that the brain in the midst of her golden beauty was remorselessly thinking, and there was no way of getting to know what passed. She understood that he wished to read her some lines of Horace that he had translated, hoping, no doubt, to win a moment of consent from her; but he had come by the wit to realize that its pure cadences would be mere uncouthness, its subtle climax a rude explosion, in the delicate silence in which she had wrapped herself.

The evening glow faded, and she heard Hubert suddenly push back his chair in the sitting-room downstairs, walk across the room and snap on the light. She stirred. Roland murmured her name, "Judith," and sought to hold her more closely. But he woke in her no sign of life. She resisted the summons to her senses; she made herself dead to him, knowing that the vision that was now dawning on her spirit would demand self-dedication, if she was going to accept it, and denial of the world.

She heard spoken words. "Do for heaven's sake speak," he was urging her. "Or kiss me, or something, to show me I'm still existing." His right hand was at his forehead. "Am I a ghost, or what?" he was exclaiming. She gave him a kiss, imitating passion, and resumed her debate. It remained to settle a number of doubts; whether she was sane; whether a state of mind is real; whether it would be worth while to follow out her experience; whether it would not be wiser to reject the kingdom of the imagination and enjoy the palpable world; whether, on the other hand, an experience might not be all, and the world nothing. It was the cold moment of a creative artist who has conceived unreasonable beauty; of a soul that has received, mystically, an absurd enlightenment.

She became aware that he was shaking her. It was treatment that she rather liked, ordinarily; but now she hotly resented it, and "Don't!" she cried.

"For God's sake, tell me what's wrong!" he insisted. "Is anything the matter? Has something funny happened?"

Something funny! Her face burned in the darkness. Her experience, if she told it, would certainly be thought funny; it would be received with unbelief and derision, like the dreams of poets that they convey in ridiculous verse. How poets must distrust themselves as they write the stuff down, she said to herself; or at least, afterwards. She was not thinking of Horace when she thought of poets, but of Shelley and Keats (wild men of the mind, her lover used to call them). Then, aloud:

"Nothing's the matter at all."

"Then why do you seem so strange?'

"Do I?" How did these things come out? Was her vision marked, somehow, on her face? Had it altered her eyes?

"You seem so far away from me," he pleaded, and clasped her as close as possible, as if seeking to crush separation between their hearts.

At once she let all her doubts go. The actual world, the smell of a tweed jacket, Roland: these things were unquestionable. She sought refuge in the actuality of Roland, believing, as she turned to him, and saw the light of joy come into his eyes, that she had settled her questions and chosen her path.

§ XI

HAPPY as the conclusion of the evening had been, there remained for Roland a slight unpleasantness, a cause for perturbation. When Judy had gone to bed this faint flavor appears to have begun to pervade his mind; the consideration of it brought him to a state of real anxiety; and at last he mentioned the matter to Hubert, who now related the conversation, with cynical enjoyment, to his sister.

He came to her room for the purpose, bringing a scent of some expensive pomade, artificial and elegant, into the fragrance of the spring night. It was a habit of his to come and argue with her when she was in bed, if there was anything to argue about; or to talk with her, for he was fond of her, and she of him, in spite of his worldliness.

He sat on a chair by her bed, crossed his elegant and beautifully trousered legs, put his hands in his pockets and cocked his shrewd face at her.

Roland, unbusinesslike, had found it difficult to begin, he told her.

"You know, your sister's a strange young woman," was all he had been able to say.

Hubert had been sitting in the open window, fanned by the spring breeze, engaged in mastering a pamphlet issued by an insurance company competitive with the one he represented. He had glanced briefly round.

"She's loopy," he had replied with economy of effort. Then, happening to catch a glimpse of Roland's face – "Of course, I don't mean that literally. Is anything particular the matter at present?"

"Oh, nothing's the matter. Only . . ."

"Only what? Speak out, my dear fellow. You must put your case if you want me to deal with it."

"Well . . . it sounds odd . . . but I really think, you know, she fancies those plants of hers have personality. I mean, yesterday, when I happened to meet her in a plant-house, she behaved as if the damned things were like people; as if we were being overlooked and overheard."

Hubert had not shrunk from the unpleasant but obvious inference. He had looked (shrewdly, of course) at his friend. "Are you quite sure," he asked, "there wasn't some one there? I mean, naturally, a real, flesh-and-blood person. A man, in fact."

This question he enjoyed repeating to Judith, who received it without comment.

Roland had flushed. "How can you suggest a thing like that?"

"You will admit it is a possibility?"

"Yes, but your own sister. . . ."

"Things like that happen, and when they do the woman involved is quite commonly somebody's sister." But it was no use talking to a fellow who had no sense of things as they are, a fellow who allowed his mind to be obscured by his desires, even to the point of a marriage that he could not afford. He glanced at her as he repeated this, but she made him no concession. "One ought to regulate things better," his discourse to Roland had continued. "So many fools have married on behalf of the prudent, and it is additionally gratifying to enjoy what another has laid up for himself." This he particularly liked telling her.

"I do not think, in point of fact, that what I suggest is the case," he had then said to Roland. "I agree with you – I think she's a bit funny sometimes. Not really loopy, you know, but I find in my experience that few people are quite sound on every point, and

Judy is rather further from the normal, on most points anyway, than most people." This he repeated to Judy with comments for her own ear.

"Is there anything to be done about it?" Roland had asked. He knew that Hubert was a practical fellow, who would always know what to do.

"There is nothing to be done, yet," Hubert had replied. "Not yet." He pondered something further. Really, he had reflected, some men are very ignorant, or blind; and sometimes one has to enlighten them – one really has to in the interests of general sanity.

"When are you going to be married?" he had asked. "Soon, isn't it?"

"June," answered Roland. Nothing seemed to have been conveyed to him. Oh! well, then – "The function of women in the world," Hubert had explained to him, "is to bear children."

When he had repeated this to Judy, and seen that her mouth was open, showing sharp little teeth, and her eyes beginning to flash topaz lightnings, he left the room abruptly.

§ XII

THERE had been some idea of spending April in Italy. In the morning Judy stated that this had become her definite intention. Within two days all arrangements were made and she was off with her mother and Roland. They did not come back until early May.

In Italy there had been no trouble. For Roland it was all sunshine, darkened only on some rare occasions by a sharp wind of irony. He obviously began to feel that the shining little piece in delphinium blue or amber yellow who created such a sensation in the Italian hotels was really his possession; he began to be proud. It was natural, then, that he should show some slight sign of distress when, within a minute of the return home she had sprung up the stairs and was standing in the summer splendors of the fern-window. It must have been odd to see her standing there in an elegant slip of a frock and modish hat, instead of in corduroys. Only the saffron flames of hair curled out in front of her ears to remind him that nature is unquenchable.

Seeing his doubts she reassured him with a smile. She had chosen the path she was going to take. She was going to give up her work in the Gardens. They would be married in less than a month, and she was going to embrace the life of any ordinary suburban young wife of beauty and intelligence – whatever sort of life that may be.

Lying straight and still once more in her own airy bedroom, she sank into a still sleep on that intention. But through all those days in Italy unknown processes had been taking place in her mind, and in the morning they came to the surface. With daybreak it was clear that one need not resign everything at once; one need not hesitate to pay just one more visit to the Gardens for the purpose of saying good-bye; indeed, one found in oneself the energy, even a certain eagerness, to review the whole situation, in order to reapprove one's decision once more.

She lay under a coverlet of peacock blue staring at the first flame-point of dawn that woke in a crystal hanging on a bracket. In that moderate, solid, and comfortably furnished house her bedroom was like a precious cabinet or shrine for a golden image. The walls glimmered with the blue of a butterfly's wings and crystals hung on silver brackets; the ceiling had the warmth of a sunrise; the windows were eastward so that the daybreaks of spring and summer flowed in like seas and drowned her in tingling splendors. Images and scenes rose before her eyes as she stared at the streak of fire in the crystal.

In a month's time, she dreamily thought, it might not be so easy to lie in bed creating scenes and pictures. That required solitude. Anxiety stirred under her heart, as she remembered how she loved the white mists of spring and summer in her bedroom – the long delicious lonelinesses, the expectances in the scented darkness, the experiences of an indescribable whispering beauty, the trances in which she found something beyond pleasure. Her brain woke. She saw plainly that she did not want to be married; that is, she corrected, to be made to live constantly in close association with Roland. In the institution of marriage she now clearly perceived the whole gross-fingered incapacity of mankind for any subtlety in the manipulation of its affairs.

And as to love – nobody had yet shown her how to be in love. In the splendid mornings of May she regretted it. She desired to be in love, and if some one should teach her . . . this means, she pointed out to herself, that you are not virtuous: it cannot, however, be helped. Perhaps, as Roland fears, you really are an artist; one who accepts all experiences.

On this view of her nature, she saw that it would be idle to resist a desire that, as she now confessed, was vigorously calling. Not omitting to remember that there were experiences she had feared, hitherto, to accept, she slid from her bed and considered further measures as she brushed her hair in the dim mirror with a great tortoiseshell brush. She longed for the bath; her arms ceased moving while she pictured the flood of warm crystal sliding into the porcelain, in the light of daybreak. But it was important not to wake the household – and in any case the water would be stone cold at that shivering hour. Four o'clock, her watch said. Not too much time for what she was minded to do; but enough. She quivered like a narcissus in wind as she thought of the beauty that she must be about to experience. She stood for a few seconds in the window, stilled by the languid splendors that were in attendance about the door of the sunrise. She could see the tops of great stately trees in the Gardens, melting southward into a delicacy of rose-madder and water-blue. She imagined the dim lawns, the rhododendrons saluting the sun, and her heart leapt with passionate longing for them. In a minute, in a minute I shall be there, she said, struggling with the silken rope of her pajamas. At last the knot gave, and a faint dawn-breeze played on her body. It was delicious, but she could not delay. Very hastily she pulled on the long silken stockings and slipped into the imponderable matters that she had discarded with her dance frock last night; over these her corduroys – and strange and heavy they seemed after a month's disuse. Then she went by way of a drainpipe to the roof of a shed, and so escaped into the sunrise.

§ XIII

THE policeman who saw her gliding along the Lower Kew Road was puzzled, but he let it go at that. He probably knew she was something to do with the Gardens, a student or gardener going to work very early, perhaps; or he may have decided that the bright-headed phenomenon was outside the scope of his duty. Others, abroad at that hour, were openly inquisitive. But at the Bridge she ran down to the towpath and sped along by the slow, sunrise-bearing river, unpursued, until she was opposite the Gardens. But then, how to cross the ditch – an impossible jump? She hunted about for a passage, remotely aware, back of her consuming intention to get into the Gardens, of a check. She was not baffled for long. A tree trunk offered what might have been thought advantages by a squirrel. She swarmed it and passed into the Gardens by means of a jutting branch, hand over hand, with swinging feet. The difficulty enraged her. One might have heard the indignant gasps that came from her chest. But in two minutes she was coursing over the grass, standing with bare head before the mountain-wall of trees, lifting her mouth to the flood of daybreak that surged over them.

At this strange hour the sky, the trees, all the lineaments of the world that grew from the mists of rose-madder and pale blue, were unreal. The air was full of a dim shimmer of birdsong, that mounted as the daylight increased and streamed in ever stronger pulsations from the invisible hearts of the bushes, from morning-bright chapels aloft in the cedars. The leaves sang. The universe was all an infinity of little green singing flames, each pointed leaf burning momently brighter, until the material world seemed to dissolve and float away in a wrack of flame and song.

With it, too, there was a dissolution in Judith. When a certain faintness, that arose from the excess of beauty, had passed, she found herself with means of knowing the plants and all that was going on around her – the drawing of food from the air, of water

33

from the soil, the exchange of substances through the conductive region of the trunk, the transpiration of watery vapors through the pores of the leaves. The physiological processes she felt dimly, as she felt the inward changes of her own body: the action of their mechanical tissues she felt just as she felt the action of her own muscles. And certain other processes, analogous to the spiritual processes in man, she quite intimately perceived. Gazing up at the glowing blossoms of the chestnut, each blossom, she imagined, an almondy bower on a mountain side, she felt suddenly the alpine spirit and magnificent exultation of the tree. Advancing a little, she saw ahead of her, in the shadowy clefts of those green mountains, a mass of rhododendrons, white and red, and joined in their solemn adoration as they held their great lanterns to the rising sun. Then it entered her head that she must see and possess all the beauty of the place in the intimacy and wonder of that hour. The day was advancing quickly. The new sunlight lay on the open lawns in fine tissues of gold, although there was still dew in the long shadows of the bushes. She sped, therefore, from point to point, coursing like some golden fawn of the daybreak, leaving her slot in grass and sandy path and meadow of bluebells; and at this point she stopped with beating heart before hawthorn; at that before magnolia, lilac, broom, or irises in a bed: and at every point it seemed to her that she was saluted by the flowers; that some fair rhododendron smiled at her, shyly, like a Greuze girl; or a tulip bowed good-morning with high and disdainful neck. How gracefully they sprang, some of the plants! How splendid was the strong thrust of stalk or branch! With what lovely consideration did the great trees dispose their masses! And when at last she stood in the circle of the azalea garden, the flowers leapt and swirled about her like flames about the stake, delicate flames of love that desired to martyr her; and a wind blew with the ardor of their passion in it, and she opened her jacket, offering her lily bosom to their fierce tongues.

§ XIV

WHEN she was satisfied of that experience, she allowed her eye to be caught by a glitter of glass, eastward, under the risen sun. Tropical friends lived there, she reflected; and they too must receive a visit. But as she wandered that way, she found herself a little tired, a trifle sobered. Some vague consciousness of her state of mind stirred in her brain, and a vague thought of Roland, of Roland as an intruder. She permitted herself a little ironical smile. In that mood she gave but perfunctory glances at her acquaintance in the great palm-house, and further on, among the tropical ferns, the temperate flowers and the economic plants. She passed the orchids and pitcher plants, and thoughtfully considered the question of the cactuses. She was very reluctant to enter the plant-houses. Strange things had happened to her that morning, and things yet stranger might happen with the addition of heat and silence and magical glass. There were extremes of experience to which she was not yet ready to give herself.

Her body was tired out, and she sought to rest herself by leaning against the jamb of the glass door that gave on the tropical lily tank. She began to think long involved thoughts, her eyes fixed on the green-bladed shafts of Thalia geniculata, by the edge of the water, bright strokes in the midst of that emerald world. It was very hot in there, and the plants were opening their vivid, bladed leaves in a silence as of some equatorial noon. Her imagination went out of her, as she rested, and wandered in the plant-world, not boldly, for her naked soul had become very sensitive to an impression of presences watching and considering. The damp atmosphere became oppressive with its burden of invisible beings. Was it possible that the imaginations of the flowers could also go forth from them to enter into conversation with some third part of her, freed in a rare sleep of the body and mind? The scene had changed a little while she was pondering. Now she seemed to be

on the shore of some lagoon in Southern India, a sheet of water
bordered by a palm-forest, covered with budding water lilies and a
delicate tracery of small floating leaves, and already, though it was
early morning, the sun burned intolerably in a tinted sky. It was
her custom, in reverie, to people the world with her own creations.
They arose, doubtless, in memory; but it was some reservoir more
remote and secret than memory that furnished the figures of this
dream. For she found herself in the midst of a strange drama, in
which there was an action without limbs and words spoken without a voice. There was before her a Being, arising, it seemed, from
the scarcely opened bud floating on the lagoon, whom she must
recognize and name the Water Lily, a personality that emerged
from the flower, a pure, intellectual and elegant spirit, meditative
and destined to sadness.

There were words in her brain that seemed to have been woken
there by some ray of thought, or desire, that proceeded from the
flower – "Float here beside me."

Even in her dream, if dream it was, she smiled; and stood out of
the dream and smiled at herself as an object in it. For she was conscious of a very human inhibition. "How absurd!" she reflected,
as she began to slip out of her clothes. "But to be naked before a
flower . . . this flower, at any rate, this pale and spiritual Being."

A swarm of small fishes in the lagoon, darting from some
gloomy lair under the tracery of leaves, flashed back the burning
sun with their golden bodies, and her soul longed for the water.
But now others were watching her. A green, palmlike emanation
made her feel as if she were being stared at, and there seemed to
be a thronging, among the tree trunks, of dark and Indian forms.
And was that a flower-hand clutching at a silken garment, or one
of those small monkeys that gibbered in the palm-forest? But a
dusky and lovely creature, the person of some precious rose from
a Rajah's garden, was at her side smiling and flushing. "You are
so beautiful and so new," were the words that woke in her mind.
"That is why they regard you, these vulgar ones." For answer she
kissed the scented and intoxicating creature.

The thoughts of the Water Lily floated from him, as it were, like an aroma. "Hide yourself near me in the water. Great beauty is not for the vulgar, but for the cultivated. The spectacle of what is beautiful, what is new, what is sad, is not for the gross."

Was there petulance, contempt, resentment in the nature of this spirit? Some trace of the passions of the plant-body?

"Ah, but indeed," came to her from the Rose, "such crystal and radiant beauty has never yet been given to us."

Now she looked down at her body, and saw the truth of those images that had been whispered to her in another world, for indeed her flesh was of the texture and purity of a flower. She had come to be half of their world. The southern sunlight was more radiant and intimate to her. Her bare feet were kissed by little feathery plants that swarmed down to the lagoon. Delighted, tingling from the sun, she stepped into the water and was in conversation with the Lily, swimming and floating and entwined with the limbs of plants, and a crocodile drowsing there ignored her. But suddenly all that was human of her seemed about to drown in this queer region of being, and she clung in a panic to any chance straw of conversation.

"Do you exist?" she asked abruptly.

He seemed to ponder. "That is a question. Would it not be difficult to say what it is to exist?" Now the lagoon and the glowing sun and his answers became more dreamlike. "How can one be certain that another exists, or indeed that there is any self? But you can be certain, in a sense, that I exist as I appear to you, for you have made me in this form within the world of your consciousness, and you are to this extent my Creator."

Her senses flew to the forest. If there were orchids there, what lovely, what irresistible beings could be imagined! She silenced her thoughts. "You can act?" she queried, with some reminiscence of the thoughts silenced. "You can effect your will?"

"The actions of this being whom you have created," he said, "are predestined in your imagination. I am, but to an extent I am in your mind. Consequently I am to an extent conditioned by your will. This is in a way captivity – charming, but still captivity."

There seemed to be something elegant, as well as philosophical, in the dreaming of this flower. She knew well that his acts, his growing up through the warm water out of ancient mud towards the fierce tropical sun, all the functioning of his plant-body, were an affair of chemistry and mechanics: she had not expected this spiritual corona – why not, she asked herself, since we have one too?

Once more he woke up a little fire of words in her mind. "The responsibility of creation is important, and the world is defective in more than one respect."

"Defective?" she wondered.

His passionate emotion spired up like a rare incense. "Existence is so beautiful and so short, subject to such melancholy disasters; the burning god who calls us from the sweet darkness of the waters to worship him, and fills our bodies with the tingling substance of life, himself slays us as a fair sacrifice."

"And sweet and faint is the lily-scent, and heavy the water-scent," she murmured.

The pale spirit became as it were clouded with his lily-anger. "Aye, and it is to be seen that this is a daughter of the burning god, a flower from the sun. Dewy one! you that shake the morning from gleaming petals, and at your blossoming there is a stirring of the song of birds! Deity, with your fragrant and golden beauty, your eternal and careless youth, your unpitying creativeness . . . !"

But she was tired of philosophizing; a little tired of play-acting. She made her way to the shore, therefore, and stood among the tendrils of myriophyllum. But now the sun in the tinted Indian sky became more sinister, the atmosphere heavier and more oppressive, laden with watching presences. There was a passing of thoughts, and a lurking in the palm-forest. Then, as she began somewhat hurriedly to find some way of escape from this place, she seemed to be seized, there was a foul breathing on her neck, and she was in the paralysis of an evil dream. Recognizing the spiny arms that had captured her, she screamed. Then a green, turbaned appearance looked into her face. . . .

"Really!" protested the Lily. "Really . . . !"

"Oh, help me!" she cried, terror-stricken. "Help me!"

"Pathological," the Lily observed, and seemed to be considering what, if anything, ought to be done. "If the power of thought . . ." But now a white and radiant Being started from among the trees, tore the green nightmare away and hurled him into the lagoon.

What he did there was not of interest to Judy; her eyes were all for that fatal Flower. The Indian sun itself seemed to burn in his body; his flesh was dazzling sunlight imprisoned in Himalayan snow. And his eyelids were violet and passionate, his gaze ardent.

"I would like to thank you," she faltered.

"Permit me," he replied, and tipped up her chin and kissed her mouth with a sort of seraphic boldness. He then vanished among the palms.

She stood looking after him, entirely filled and captured by an inexpressible warmth and sweetness. Then, suddenly coming to her ordinary senses, she realized that she was still outside the greenhouse, gazing through the door with her lips pressed to the glass.

§ XV

BY mid-day she was wondering whether there was anything wrong with her – that day-dream had been so vivid, so real. But also so sweet! At lunch-time, sniffing the commonplace aroma of mincemeat, she decided, on an empty stomach, to see a psycho-analyst. It was obvious, however, what any psycho-analyst would say. His conversations followed one another through her head.

But what have I done, she asked herself, other than create as a poet does? Is that pathological? She decided that she felt thoroughly fit, except that there was a marked distaste for Roland, and a sinking feeling in the chest, a disconcerting spasm in the region of the heart, a thrilling convulsion of the nerves, whenever she remembered the eyes of that Orchid.

At work in the afternoon nothing happened; everything was quite ordinary. She did not expect anything; she was busy thinking over her daybreak vision and wondering if there was any way of getting rid of Roland for a week or two. She feared Roland was bound to come in the evening. Could she go to bed with a headache? If she did, Roland would come to her room and be distressed and sympathetic (but rather more distressed – or, perhaps, impatient – than sympathetic). No means of getting rid of Roland occurred to her.

He came, and she was cold. She found it quite impossible to evoke in herself one single thrill of the nerves. He seemed tedious beside the Lily, infinitely plain beside the Orchid (and the only response that he got from her lips was when she suddenly remembered the glorious mouth of that flower).

The evening, from both their points of view, was a total loss; at nine o'clock she yawned her desire for sleep, and Roland stamped his foot in what seemed to her a merely pettish despair.

"I'm sick of asking what's the matter with you!" he cried.

"Nothing's the matter," she replied, suddenly convinced, in the glamour of twilight, that her vision was reasonable.

"Well, what do you want to go to bed for?"

"I'm very tired," she answered, not wishing to say that she had been up at daybreak, or that she was going to be up at daybreak to-morrow (and she must spend the night there sometime, to make acquaintance with the night-flowering plants).

"You're not tired," he said, "you merely don't love me."

"Yes I do, silly." She kissed him, trying once again to lend a little flavor to her kiss by remembering the Orchid. But she could not remember him voluntarily.

"You do not love me," he repeated.

"Oh well then," she replied, seeing a chance and tentatively grasping it, "perhaps after all I don't. . . . Oh yes I do, I know I do," she added hastily. "I mean to marry you . . . to be your wife . . . in June, in a month . . . or perhaps in July . . . or August . . . at any rate, this summer . . ."

He refused to believe her, and she went to bed, leaving him black and brooding.

§ XVI

LATER, Hubert came to her room. She set her teeth, determined to resist his appalling common sense till the last.

"What's this I hear about putting off your wedding?" he began.

She had her own methods of evading his inquisition. No use to deny or protest. "And supposing I decide not to marry at all?" she suggested. "Why should a woman marry?"

He ignored this tempting question for the moment; it was not one of those occasions for arguing academically with her far into the night. "What you've got to do, my girl, is to marry, and to marry at once."

"Why should a woman marry when she is economically independent?"

"You are not economically independent." He stuck ruthlessly to the actual case. "True, you make something with your journalism, but that's not independence, for you."

"What is it when added to Roland's money?"

"Something paltry," he answered shortly. "Nothing less than ten thousand a year is an income."

"You want me to marry a poor man, then. Why don't you wait until some one rich wants to marry me?"

"Because I want you off my hands. If I did wait you'd only get some other silly fancy in your head, and I should have this trouble all over again. No, my girl; you're going to marry Roland and I'm going to see you do it, and when you're married I'll take Roland and put a few grains of sense into him and make him turn his talents into something lucrative. I'll make him dress well, to start with. No man can do anything successfully who isn't well turned out."

"Your proposal doesn't attract me. The more Roland gets, the less what I have will seem, and the more dependent on him I shall be."

"My dear, good idiot, the point is not, for the moment, that you should be economically independent; the point, for the moment, is that you should marry. A woman isn't sane until she's married. It isn't nature for a woman to be economically independent . . ."

"I merely don't agree," she interrupted, shivering because her brain examined his proposition with signs of a disposition to perceive truth in it. To an artist all propositions seem true.

"When you're married you'll see that," he went on. "You'll drop a lot of nonsense when you're married, and a lot more when you find you're going to have a baby."

"Who said we were going to have a baby?" she parried. "As a matter of fact" – she felt strangely uncovered and helpless and childish as she said it – "as a matter of fact we're not."

He looked at her with speculation. "Don't tell me," was his conclusion.

"We're not," she protested, still more confused, but hiding it.

He looked again shrewdly. "My dearest Judy, you are my sister, and of course to me you are more or less ordinary; but let us examine the facts and the probabilities. . . ." And he talked to her with brotherly disinterestedness.

"That's enough out of you," she said, looking at him as indifferently as possible from under her hat of fire.

"Yes," he said. "You may have cold, calculating eyes, like a cat's; but you are a sensationalist like a cat too, and what I say is right. It always is!"

She caught hold of his sleek hair and pulled it until he pinched her ribs so hard that she had to leave go. It was a friendly tussle such as they were accustomed to, but with a slight added pinch of seriousness, and even, on her part, of temper.

"I won't have children till I'm a hundred," she told him. "Not till I'm so old that I don't mind giving up my own individual life and letting them have it instead."

"Theory," he observed.

What was she to put up by way of defense? Somehow, with Hubert, no proposition seemed to hold water but his own.

"Your views about women," she observed, "are all founded on

one specious book by a strutting rooster. He's a cock crowing on a doorstep, that man; the conceited cockbird ridiculously telling us all what he's done. You have also some experience with the emptier-headed kind of girl. You gravitate towards them, naturally, because they can't answer you back: just as some men gravitate towards those who don't resist anybody, and then boast of their conquests and say that all women can be obtained."

"I like you in this mood," he answered. "I like you when you talk wittily about the world, about what is. You have some knowledge of human nature. I have more. Should I be right if I guessed that some other man has come along and supplanted Roland, as they say, in your affections?"

"You would not," she replied, with glad promptitude.

He was just a little taken aback. "Well, something's biting you," he said at last, "and I shall find out quickly enough what it is. I advise you to marry Roland; marry him at once. Take my advice and you'll find you'll be happy. A woman needs a man she can hang on to, and nothing goes right till she gets one. Will you take my advice?"

"Probably not."

"If you don't I shall certainly do something about it." He took his hands out of his pockets and stood up. "I give you a month to decide."

"What infernal cheek!" she exclaimed, staggered, but he was already outside the door.

What was she to do, if she could use neither her beauty nor her brains successfully against him? And what would he do on his part? There was nothing that could be efficacious to deprive her of what she desired.

§ XVII

ON a hot morning towards the end of May she sat wearily on the stone edge of the Water Lily tank, eating her sandwiches. The plant-houses were empty of visitors, for it was lunch-time. The Gardens were aflame with the full splendors of May, but she was unhappy, for an invisible barrier seemed to have been interposed between herself and the plant-world. She had tried many ways of repeating the state she had been in that morning, including alcohol, but all was in vain; and now even her work was unsatisfying and fruitless, her experiments lacked inspiration, and her drawings were dead. The way into the plant-world was lost, and perhaps it had never existed, save in illusion. If so, life held out no attractions, and there was nothing for it but the impending marriage with Roland. But how wonderful that would have been, she thought, feeling some stir of the May, if Roland could be changed into the starry person of that Orchid. She had known now for one moment at the waking end of a dream how love enters the body like a sweet madness, and changes the world.

She sighed, sitting among reeds by the waters of a river, tears for the lost kiss of that passionate flower started to her eyes; a mocking voice floated to her like an emanation from the pale, meditative Lily.

"Have you borrowed those dew diamonds from the small leaves of Salvinia auriculata, as a gift of jewels for that faithless lover?"

There was now no semblance of the Lily: nothing but the white cup on the stream and the cold, floating words as of a voice; a communion established in a world of green stalks and blades between her being and the being of this flower.

"Tell me," she eagerly answered, "about your life."

"Life is disastrous."

The voice did not remember her: it was but one of a myriad opening lily buds that spoke for all lilies: they had no individuality, perhaps, no memory – or but a fugitive soul and a faint memory like a fading scent.

"Life is very short, very sad."

Now thoughts came to her from another quarter, where the Sacred Fig, the Fig of Krishna, was dreaming:

"If any spirit hath opened to the sun of the Supreme, the Infinite; that is neither living nor lifeless; that cannot be described, yet it abounds in means and objects of satisfaction; that dwells not in perishable cells and tissues of stem or leaf, but within its essential nature, inconceivable, unsurpassed; root, leaf and flower of the universe, begetting itself from itself; possessing the attributes of purity, beauty and irresistible splendor: that spirit knoweth how we may escape from existence and, when we fade, fade forever into the Supreme, the Infinite. For the desire of the sun and of seeding, all the illusory pleasures of projected existence. . . ."

"Tedious, isn't it?" agreed the Water Lily to her sigh. "This Supreme, this Infinite – what is it but a consolation? The Supreme is Nothing. When we fade, we fade – we that flower to one pulsation of the sun, struggling for a brief flame-point of individuality – into the unconscious bosom of Nothing, who pays no heed to desire. But it is blindly ordained that while we flower we shall reproduce: and this is our fate, the fate of our generation, to flower and reproduce and fade; and so it shall be with us and our successors to the end of time. As to the doctrine of this Fig – I despise it!"

"I have no objection to his doctrine," she said; "it was only that I was desiring to see another Shape." And she looked vainly through the emerald jungle of reeds and deep-bladed trees for that tropical splendor.

Now the form of the Water Lily arose from the flower and stood clearly before her, hovering over the river, and there was in the midst of him a most delicate flush of pink: – "Ah!" he seemed to convey: "That Orchid! That love-engine! That epiphyte!" The pink flush faded. "Let me tell you that the hopes and pleasures attaching to the processes of inflorescence and pollination are the most cruel of illusions."

"He is certainly unsentimental, this pallid flower," she thought.

His answer proceeded. "If the Water Lily is indifferent to hope, attaches no value to sentimentalities, seems ruthless and formidably cold, the Water Lily has copied reality. The Water Lily is the icy truth in flower."

"But there is also a moment of delicate poetry, this pure flush of pink in the tip of the white petal. You are unsentimental, no doubt; but I do not find you formidable, and I doubt, really, whether you are cold."

His semblance shrank. "Nevertheless, you perhaps assent to
that truth of the Universe that I express in my form and nature – a
purity arising from mud, and flowering into annihilation."

"Oh!" she replied, "I will assent to anything that is well or
charmingly argued."

He became very still, as if he would give consideration to
something. He seemed to enjoin repose. "Attend once more to the
Sacred Fruit."

Again thoughts came from the Fig: "All creatures that live are
subject to grief, because of their desire. Grief issues from desire,
and pleasure from grief, and grief again from pleasure. Pleasure
and grief are an eternal cycle of seed and flower, flower and seed."

"I gather," said Judy, "that this world of yours is not, as I had
supposed, one where every individual is happy in the simple fulfill-
ment of function?" Warm and sweet-smelling was the earth, the
moist pebbles; delicate the reed-smell, heavy the leaf-smell. She
had thought it desirable to inhabit this warm, moist and scented
universe.

It was the Water Lily who replied. "Happy! Did you imagine
the plants were not sensitive to pain; that they did not suffer in the
physical disasters of which they are daily in danger? Happy! in a
world where the struggle for life is such that if you relax one nerve,
one cell, for an instant, some thrusting neighbor will obtain your
place in the light? A world where loathsome parasites are everywhere seeking for your vitals! A world in which you are the food
of noisome snails and other creatures . . . !"

The words of the Priest now superseded the Lily's in her
thoughts: "As in the vast regions of the air one speck of dust meets
another, and they drift apart, such is the pollination of flowers. It is
not well to hope, and to pine for love, for in the instant of meeting
there must be a parting. Thou and that other shall be united but by
a flying speck, and both must shortly return into the Infinite, the
Supreme. . . ."

"This Supreme, this Infinite," she mused, "is a disagreeable sort
of thing, and really very much the same as the Water Lily's cold
truth."

That flower resumed his complaint. "A world, finally, in which vegetables have lost the dominion. For now are we increasingly subject to a dimly felt oppression of capricious presences. . . ."

She interrupted his thoughts with thoughts of her own. For had she not been oppressive and capricious with the knife and the electric probe? Had she not experimented with anesthetic and poison? Did she not know that the plants lived in the very machines with which she measured their responses?

These thoughts belonged to the specifically human part of her constitution, and the human part of her was waking. The Water Lily withered before her eyes; the Fig of Krishna became a plant in a pot; the tinted firmament took shape as a wall of glass; she returned to her proper condition, disappointed and angry. "You have learned nothing of the life of plants!" she told herself, shaking her golden head. All those thoughts she herself must have invented – but out of what unknown part of her did these imaginations proceed? Out of what secret store of experience did she clothe what were perhaps, after all, plant realities in human language?

§ XVIII

"WHAT a fool you are!" She plagued herself, dragging home tired and hungry, in the growing heat of the summer's afternoon. She had abandoned her work.

"A student of botanical science; the reputed possessor of a critical intelligence – enamored of an imagined Orchid!" She laughed suddenly in the face of an early clerk who was passing; and he faltered in his tracks, mortally wounded.

"How can it happen so easily?" she questioned. "Really, if I should imagine him again, and if he should offer to kiss me, I must . . ." But what she must do was left undecided, for she was trying to recall his appearance. It was not quite easy, for in this waking mood he had to resemble a human being more closely: she had to invent a man. Still, she caught glimpses of him – savage lord of some green and temperate forest on Himalayan slopes, delicate

Rajah of some marble palace among lakes and hanging gardens and mysterious woods. So delicate and yet so fierce! So strong and yet so slender; shy, yet instant. What dazzling flesh, what a fair broad chest, and what shapely shoulders! Rhythms of the leopard lived in the muscles of head and neck; there was a quelling hint of the tiger-leap in loins and well-proportioned limbs. The mouth was sensitive, aristocratic, a trifle petulant; the eyes were long and deep and splendid. But there was melancholy on his face; a purple doom-shadow. Her heart suffered for him, and suddenly she remembered the deep violet of his eyes that had held hers, the lovely hues that had flushed his cheek, the delicate and intoxicating scent of his kiss.

"If I should imagine him again . . ." her nerves shivered . . . "kiss me he may," she said aloud; and a man passing, an irresolute-looking man, one full of unquiet doubts and half-confirmed suspicions, stopped and lingered under the wall.

"He may! He may!" she repeated. "For I did not know life held such wonder, such delight, as this experience of being incontinently in love." Her brows frowned on the sudden profound anguish of desire.

But she had turned into the lime avenue, and the picture of the lover she had so clearly imagined as she glided along (straw in mouth, the golden stable-boy!) mingled inextricably with the picture of Roland. She banished it.

She was home. On the second landing, outside the bathroom, she met Hubert in his dressing-gown, bathed and cool after the heat of the day. He looked closely in her eyes and considered the color of her cheeks. "You've been meeting some one," he accused.

"I haven't."

"You have."

"I tell you I haven't."

"Why did you go out so early this morning?"

"I went to see the Water Lilies."

"What on earth for, at that time of day?"

"Because they have to be examined in the morning. They are only fully expanded then. Didn't you know?"

He signified his complete rejection of her statements, and vanished into his room. She was left with the world of her imagination shuddering from his blatant touch. How mad to dream within herself of the kisses of an Orchid – how unbotanical! how anthropomorphic!

§ XIX

Now it was almost June, and though no clear vision had come to her for a few days she was not disturbed: she felt, now, like a spectator of events that were bound to take place in her mind, and she was prepared, now, to abandon herself almost entirely to her experiences. But not quite. She still held to some part of her human mind and would not let go. It was as if some spirit-lover demanded the full surrender of her imagination to his uses, and still she refused, clinging to human dreams. But the glory of summer increased in her the desire of beauty.

She was working, one afternoon, on questions of descent as regards the Selaginellæ. "These are proud ones, I suppose," she observed to herself. "Very old family, these. But how they must have come down in the world – from being great and stately trees to insignificant and not always particularly pretty ferns." But she was restless and expectant; increasingly, as the day wore on: sometimes, instead of working and thinking about the Selaginellæ, she found herself staring at the glowing gold moss on the trunks of the tree-ferns, or at the line where the green wall of creeper, like the wall of some old, ruined temple in a fern-forest, stood up against the glassy spaces of sky; sometimes she was on the point of conceiving an evasive, green-golden, unearthly beauty that brought to her eyes tears bright and sweet as the dew-diamonds that stand on the floating leaves of the water-ferns; sometimes she stood on tiptoe, with her hand at her heart, listening, in the heat and stalk-smell and dripping silence, for a footfall, a whispering voice, an insistent mouth.

"They are somewhere near me," she whispered, "the plant

people. On the other side of a silence. Behind the light." She half closed her eyes for the sweetness of her sensations, and the mass of ferns looked, through her eyelids, like forests hanging on the mountains, with Lygodium volubile pouring from the shoulder of the range like a cascade. Then she seemed to wander there among old cities buried in a green twilight, and for an instant she became a fern, and smelled the warm earth and took pleasure in the spray of the waterfall. "They are there on those mountains," she said, coming to herself, "so far that I can hardly see them; too far for them to hear my voice." A green aureole of maidenhair clung to a hanging basket: she took the delicate sprays in her hands, and pressed her face into the heart of the moist green cloud. Then swiftly opened her eyes and stared round her: for had there been a movement, a murmur? No. There was no movement, no murmur.

The ferns dreamed on in the stillness and heat and moist silence of the afternoon, and she considered her work. Then it occurred to her that she had a job to do among the cactuses. "Why should that suddenly occur to me?" she critically asked – and smiled, for it was nearer the lily tank, nearer the orchid house. For the minute she could think of no reason connected with her work for going to the orchids.

She transferred her attentions, then, to the cactuses, and for some time she pursued her investigations among them with fairly single mind, making an effort, perhaps, to justify the abrupt change of occupation. "I'm afraid," she said, busily handling her tools, "that I'm doing some plant an injury. But what can I do? One has to handle them thus in the interests of science ... well ... even in their own interests. It's a pity, of course, when they are young, tender ... oh!" She laid down her instrument. "How wonderful it would be to dissect an orchid! To cut one's lover open, and slit him up, and separate him part from part ... ! How would a flower like to dissect a woman?" She stopped, horrified at herself. "What an awful sort of thing I must be," she thought, trembling. "Why do I have such thoughts?" She saw herself as a ghoul, and ran from the place to escape the terrible vision of her own nature. By chance she took refuge in the orchid house.

§ XX

S HE lay hidden, drugged with the redolent heat, until the gardeners had gone, and the plant-houses were shut, and only a drip of water disturbed the silence. Then she stole out again and looked among the plants. There he was, and she forgot everything. There he was, the Orchid, with his substance of evening sunlight indwelling in frozen snow, symbol of Himalayan cold rising from tropical sunset. Gently she touched the flower with her fingers and ventured a little pinch, and threads of flame ran through her nerves from his body of white fire. Beyond him, through the glass, she saw twilight lawns and darkening tree-masses; beyond that, burning through tones of purple, a deep glory of the sun. It was very still and quiet; an extraordinary stillness and peace stole through her body, fortifying her for the onset of profound beauty. It came sudden and full. She put her two hands about the flower, and kissed the deep violet of his heart, swooning with love.

§ XXI

S HE carried the flower in her hand among evening trees, a poet shielding her spark of the heavenly fire. There was a chance. She was gliding, the golden diaphane, among dark and ancient conifers on the shore of a lake, and a dull-red planet, swimming in a warm and musky twilight, berubied the water. She stole like a scented wind through the whispering bamboo garden, seeking her lover, and there the moon hung in the sky, a golden hawk perched over a star. Now she was flitting by staircase and colonnade of marble in the gardens of some great lord: in the moonlight she dimly perceived a presence of flowers, a glimmer of amorous faces; the somber and splendid passion of love bloomed like the rhododendron. Somewhat terror-struck because of her loneliness in that ghostly palace, she passed among orange trees in a gleaming arcade where green parrots slept. And where was this? In whose gardens, and in what time? Her memory knew those gleaming terraces, those dreamy trees. They were the gardens of a prince – but who was he? Iranian conqueror in the daybreak of history; fair-haired Greek reigning in the palace of some conquered Indian; or hyacinthine immortal? Her heart was beating as an ever more vivid memory of scented kisses returned to her. But he was not there, her master. Vainly her eyes swept the great terrace that overhung a wild and enchanted water: there was nothing but silence; silence and gloomy forests out there on the mountains; moon-drenched silence more terrible because of some passionate bird that poured out song in tune with her pulses. The little balcony at the far end of the terrace was empty, save for the blue moonbeams; empty, and she must have lost her way, or forgotten some habit of her lord's, in these remembered gardens. But ah! The wild beating of her heart redoubled, for now that little balcony of marble was not quite empty; there was a form among the blue moonbeams, a flower of the moonlight, the silence, the bird's passion, the sadness of the water and the forest, the vast, cruel beauty of night. She gave a little ghost of a cry that went shivering among the marble columns: he turned, and she saw once more his cold, beautiful face, his wide and splendid eyes: at last she was in his arms, swooning with love and waking as she swooned to the remembered sweetness of his handling.

"You have been a long time," he said, when their first happiness abated. "You have kept me." His voice was grave and imperious, and she remembered how cruel this beautiful warrior and godlike master of women could be. But just now she was fain even of his anger and clung to him, saying: "I was detained. . . . I don't know . . . there was some cause why I could not come to you." It was sweet to submit herself to the mercy of his desire.

He led her to a seat, and she lay with her head on his breast, while her eyes took in the familiar mosaic of anemones on a ground of moss-green, and marble elephants, rising from the water, on whose huge shoulders the terrace rested.

"Princess and captive," he said, "you have not thanked me, to-night, that I delivered you from a tyrant. . . ."

"And brought me under this delicious tyranny." She turned her face up to him, remembering some incident – a shining and imperial figure on a horse, with attendant princes in some warlike country; the flash of swords; instant and overwhelming love.

He sought her mouth, and his princely hand had captured her breast. She met his lips coldly.

"Why do you not thank me, since the minutes speed by?" he asked with slow anger, and addressed himself once more to the task of compulsion. Yet though longing she still refused, and made him strive more amusingly for his reward. But why did he say that the moments sped? Had they not time for their love? A cloud was on her mind. "You are cruel," he murmured.

"Yes," she answered, permitting kisses.

"And capricious!" as she put an end to them.

But now she felt the surge of his wrath, and gravely set her mouth to his dazzling flesh. "Ah!" he exclaimed. "This is a danger-ous way of thanking a king!"

A king! Some word of doom echoed. She pondered a little, as she lay on his breast, and again her eyes searched those colonnades, those orchards of orange trees. Hidden there, she remembered, were little melancholy gardens, and sad rooms with mosaic of glass and porcelain – roses, she remembered, and kingfishers. There came back to her a host of sad meditations in those delicate chambers, a recollection of physical agony and some profound suf-fering of the mind: had she been tortured there by a lord whose desire had altered; or had he died? A door opened on darkness, and she shrank back into the bosom of her lover, who now seemed somewhat shadowy and spectral.

Once more his voice: "Tell me again, golden spear, of that glowing country that made this white flesh; tell me what foreign thoughts there are in those moonlit-cloud eyes."

But a sadness, a fear, had seized her. His eyes looking into hers were eyes of violet night, and in them, she knew, was a love for her enveloping and terrible as the darkness of space; his love, his cruelty and his princely coldness were of eternity and the unknown, and her individuality perished in that infinite darkness. But on him, on the lordly body that desired her fairness, lay the decree of fate. And now she saw the violet shadows of death on his countenance, and suddenly remembered their doom. The last night . . . the last time. . . . She had an inkling of imperial disasters and dynastic overthrows; she turned to him swiftly; their passion became deeper and more solemn; as their lips met they knew that when an hour should have spilled its moments there must begin for them an age-long separation. She was to pass on, from this terrace of ghostly marble, out of this sultry and magical night – where? What stranger experience awaited her? Once more she drew back, shuddering, from a blackness and abyss of the mind.

How taciturn he was; taciturn, as one who knows the futility of words in the face of doom. Nor, if this proud king and cold philosopher had asked for consolation, could she have found any language to avail with the oncoming silence. Yet suddenly he clapped his hands twice, and there was music made by the royal orchestra hidden under the terrace. He sought her fingers again, but his clasp did not tighten on her. He sat in a profound stillness, an image of pure marble gazing calmly out over the lake. His stillness lulled her into a sleep within a sleep, so that the mysterious music seemed the very voice of the lilies ascending from the water, and she was within a little of passing altogether into the body and experience of a flower. Once again that shuddering, that fear, so that her lover, aware of it, pressed her hand.

"Do not tremble," his calm voice said. "Death and darkness and the soul of the universe are kind, and we shall forget our pain."

"And our love?" She woke from her dream within a dream murmuring that question.

"Yes, death will annihilate love. Love is neither deep nor sweet, if it does not know this, and the kindness of it."

"It is not true," she said; but he smiled. "You are a woman." She only looked at him sidelong, and smiled, secretly, in her turn.

Now both were silent, listening to the mysterious water-music and gazing at the moon, the golden eagle hanging over the forests.

She lay in his arms, and sometimes his lips were on her mouth or her eyelids; but the sweetness of their passion was somewhat dim, like a memory that must not detain her, and the taste of his kisses flowed away from her, a little unheeded, on the remorseless stream of time. Once more she came near the edge of what is human: and this time she did not draw back. "I am not afraid of death," she said all at once, as a thought stole into her mind. "I await it" – but her flesh shrank from the remembered agony of the sword blade, and she glanced among the columns and orange trees – "that I may continue my journey, or else return home. For it seems to me that I am on a queer voyage. My spirit is wandering to and fro in the dark fields of time, seeking some old experience, or some new one, and it has lodged here, in these magic gardens, because of a familiar memory. But how it will quicken all my life with a fierce pain when I think of your face and your kisses!"

Her thoughts did not seem at all strange to him. "This shall cease some day," he answered, "and you shall enter the bosom of that One who does not suffer."

"That One!" She was illuminated. "That One uses me and my suffering. These are His visions, clouded with my own thoughts. Shall I give myself to Him altogether, for this last dark experience that He desires?" She pondered, until some far-away clash of weapons sent a chill to her heart. "Ah, my shadow-lord!" For the last time she swooned from his ambrosial kisses.

She clung to him, for a cry rang out, and there was a wailing in a distant part of the palace. He folded her in his arms, and she imitated his contempt, though with trembling lips, until there came a patter of naked feet on the marble, a rushing of white-clad forms, and the searing of steel in her side.

§ XXII

A MOONLIT lawn, a gleam of water, a spray of lime leaves quivering in an immensity of sky, and a dim figure on the lawn. She was not at all sure whether it was Hubert, or his specter.

He seemed spectral and thin; an image made out of the ghostly substance of moonlight, an element in the illusion of sky and lawn and dark branch of lime. Or there was a veil of moonshine between him and her, and she had passed through it into another world.

His voice came across the intervening distance, small and harsh with the cold of outer space.

"What are you doing there?"

"Nothing."

"And who is your companion?"

"Nobody," she replied.

"Nonsense! One doesn't sit with nobody doing nothing in the dark."

"Not in your world perhaps," she scoffed.

"You're mad."

"No. Only different. It's different on my side of the moonshine, that's all."

"Don't talk so strangely, for heaven's sake! There's no moonshine in my world, I can tell you, if there is in yours. Nothing but cold, hard facts. . . ."

"Glittering, moon-reflecting facts. . . ."

"Cold, hard facts, I said. And one of them is that if you find a girl under dark trees at night you'll find some one else as well, if you look hard enough. I'm going to look now. . . ."

Involuntarily she glanced back and he caught the gesture. She strove to overcome the distance between them, and achieve the sense of reality in which one can argue.

"My brother," she whispered to herself, and the world held a faint echo of meaning. She woke a little from a dream.

"What business is it of yours? What do you mean by following me about?" she cried.

He was coming towards her across the silvery lawn. He brushed past her, a ghostly hound. She stood quite still and heard him snouting in the undergrowth. The lime leaves suddenly fluttered in a slight wind, fluttered against the moon like small flags. He was at her side.

"What did you find?" she mocked.

"Nothing but this," and he pressed an orchid into her hand. "The flower he gave you, no doubt."

She stared at it, and he stared at her face.

"You flaxen Judy!" he gibed. "I can see the flush of your cheeks even by moonlight, and there's a light in your eyes that's more than the moon. A girl that looks like that has been kissed. I'll find you out, I warn you. I'll get to the bottom of this."

"And I warn you,"– she was now pale, hissing flame – "if you interfere with me I'll strike you with a madness. I'll present you with a fact that will dissolve your little hideous reasonable world into a smoke of burning electric particles. I'll teach you, poor dry-brain, wretched maimed mind that gropes along by means of brick walls, that there is strangeness and unreason in the universe. I'll . . ."

He stormed her down, but there was an uncertainty in his voice. "Be quiet! Be quiet, you tow-headed witch, and don't stare at me."

But she stared, and they challenged one another across the lawn. The lime leaves fluttered again like scented moths.

§ XXIII

THE guests went early, and while there was still a trace of daylight, about ten o'clock, she bade Roland good night – the earliest she might without making his despair inconvenient – and fled to her moth-blue room. Her heart had been thumping all dinner-time, her nerves had trembled all the heavy June evening, at the thought of the secret that her room held. After some days of doubting and hanging back, she had almost resolved, now, to reject the criticisms of her intellect and surrender herself finally, in whatever way should be demanded of her, to her own unreasonable impulse. The resolution was taken and the moment was come. To her dismay and anger, she found Hubert in her room, studying one of her notebooks in a window-seat. She snatched it from him.

"Is there no base trick that you will not play?" she asked.

He stared at her. "You are excited, you gaudy mop."

She saw herself in a mirror, still dressed for the dinner-party, a long-legged, bold child; an apparition in dress of gold, with gold helmet and shoes, a glittering and terrible fairy fetched out of the fires of the sunset.

"If I saw those shoulders on another girl," her brother continued, "I suppose I should think them fascinating. It is odd – I imagine people must be getting moral, because really you've got practically nothing on. That frock comes practically to nothing, yet nobody notices."

"My room is private," she said, with a glance into the shadows of the garden.

"I am one of the few who know what is good for people. Any steps that I take are therefore justified. I consider it to be in the interests of everybody that I should know what you are about. It is therefore necessary that I should be in possession of all the evidence, by whatever means available. That is common sense. Ordinary sound facts. It is absurd to talk about trickery."

"To-morrow," she said, "I shall leave the house and take steps to ensure that you cannot follow me."

"Useless," he said. "A girl is helpless without a man; and as far as I can gather from your conversation it's not a man you've got, but a Nobody."

His impertinence was not defensible, she felt; his case was weak in the extreme; yet she felt helpless against him. There was no way of preventing his actions, misconceived and blind though they were. She could not even have turned him out of her room, anxious as she was to be alone, because he had more muscle than she.

"Will you please let me have my room to myself," she commanded.

"As there is nothing further to be gained by staying, I will go." But he turned at the door, and sniffed, and searched the room with his inquisitive gaze. "What is the strange scent?" His nose sniffed a delicate plant-scent that floated in on the June air.

"Hang it!" he exclaimed. "What is the mystery that clings

to you? The house seems full to-night of some queer presence. Judith! Have you got some one hidden here?" He began to search, but in her wrath she made a gesture that stopped him.

"Why can't you tell us what it's all about?" he asked, arrested, puzzled.

"Will you please leave me."

She was possessed, for she had submitted herself to the inspiration of some profound interior will, whose majesty shone in her body and shamed him at last. He left the room.

She locked the door after him, thrust off her clothes in one sweep, and sank into the window-seat, trembling and doubting. Outside, on the sill, stood an orchid in a pot, an orchid made out of the substance of starlight with deep suffusions of some heliotrope element. For background, the tree-tops, and fountains of lightning among summer clouds.

"Ah!" she exclaimed, intoxicated with the heat and the June scents, "I want you!" She understood what desire was, at last, in the climax of June: her senses lived like tuned strings: she knew love.

She wished that the waves of passion would close over her, that she might drown and find an oblivion; but no vision arose. "Orchid! Orchid!" she sighed, not knowing by what name to call her lover, and put her mouth to the flower's heart; but she could raise up nothing sharper than a memory, and one that became dimmer the more she tried to possess it. Perhaps it was because of her anger with Hubert – her nerves could not forget. Perhaps not in this house: possibly the imagination was chilled to inactivity by his neighborhood, and it was thus that he had frozen her dream when he found her in the Gardens. Her mind flew to the Gardens, the moonlit plant-houses, and she began a little thoughtfully to handle her clothes. Thoughtfully, because she feared what the ghostly beauty of those plant-houses on a summer night might do to her. But it was useless to stay here, cajoling a memory. She said to herself what she had not intended to say; a sentence came from a region of her that had been forgotten: "It would be better to be with Roland."

She pulled back the peacock-blue coverlet of her bed, and the white sheet, and lay down to consider her state of mind.

Outside the window, against brooding summer trees, the image of her shadowy flower-lover had some features of the image of Roland. How queer if it should be Roland who reaped the advantage of her vision; if she should have learned in the arms of a shadow to desire a man!

"Beast!" she exclaimed, thinking of Hubert; for now she was in the midst of contending forces, and it was he who had spoilt her peace. She lay and stared at the summer lightnings that glimmered in hanging crystals and gave a bluish shine to the walls, while thoughts that she did not want took possession of her. "It won't do." She decided to seek refuge from her thoughts, and the stuffy heat, and the loneliness and unprolific silence: she would visit the plants. She began to dress, and was standing by the window, still faintly doubtful and in fear of the brooding trees and the unearthly splendor of June, when she heard whispers on the landing. There was a crack of light under the door. That was Hubert's voice, and her mother's frightened exclamation. And Roland? What part was he playing? Roland was there too, but urgently protesting.

A bang. "Unlock the door," said Hubert's voice. Then, "She has some one there, I'm certain!" The door shook.

She made no answer, and quietly slipped into her frock. Then, riding the window-sill, she looked back at the glimmering room, the patches of dusky blue and snowy white where her bed was, the crack of light under the door. The flowerpot slipped from her hand and crashed on the tiles below. At that the door was shaken with vigor. "Good-bye, little fool!" she whispered, for Hubert.

Presently, from the garden, she heard her door give. There was an irruption of light into her bedroom and heads appeared at the window. Hubert's voice floated clearly down:

"She has gone to the Gardens. I'll follow her."

Then Roland, from far away – she swiftly understood that he had refused to enter her bedroom: "She is not to be followed. I absolutely will not allow it."

She escaped from the garden with the broken flower in her
hand.

§ XXIV

THE night was heavy-scented, unearthly, a little ominous.
Massive clouds moving along the horizon were charged with
pale gleams and faint rumblings; thoughts of a god overcast with
sultry and thunderous music. She scarcely recollected her flight,
now: she only remembered an escape into shadowy valleys among
tree-masses that shone in the moon like shoulders of mountains;
and it seemed to her, as she emerged from those ghostly passes,
that she was accompanied by voices of flowers. She was alone,
save for certain presences, on the space of a lawn; long banks of
rhododendron gathered in the moonlight with the surge and spurt
of breaking rollers; branches of lightning quivered in brooding
clouds and shone in the distant dome of the palm-house.

The ghost of her Orchid lover was pleading: "You will come to
me! You will not pass me by"; and perhaps his proud face showed
a little anxiety, lest her spirit should drift from his in the limbo of
free-floating memories.

"Yes! Oh yes! I desire your kisses!" Hurriedly she held out, in
the moonlight, a hand that was not taken, and pressed on towards
the plant-houses. It was there that she was to receive the ultimate
experience; and she must not listen too long to the whispers of a
sad, pleading memory. Yet, in the flicker of a lightning flash, she
saw as it were the glorious beauty and dazzling splendor of a face,
so that her heart stopped and she must put her hands to her eyes.

She was hurrying down a wide aisle of grass, a thread of gold
blown down a night of trees. "In the shadow of the trees," she
thought, "there is a thronging of roses." Over the lake the moon
sailed, big, round and rose-yellow; ahead of her was a gleam in the
roots of the sky, a shine of glass under clouds full of lightning and
moody presences.

"Let us stay here and dream again of that old happiness; here among trees." She thought that cool fingers pinched her ear and a scented breath played on her cheek. She fluttered on, a bright roseleaf drifting.

"Or there among palms and cascading ferns." But she left the glittering palm-house on her right hand. Round as a bubble it loomed over her, full of brown gleams and indigo reflections, shining back the solemn June splendors, returning the lightnings that shivered up from cloud masses into the deep of heaven.

She let herself into the plant-houses, and stole down those corridors of glass and moonbeams like some disguised atom of the sun, creeping to see how the plants live under the reign of his mirror. She went swiftly from point to point, in an agitation, seeking an unknown circumstance that should release her spirit for an adventure that she did not know how to begin. First she passed through a scented region of orange trees and camellias. There were many flowers in that fragrant forest, suffusing the moonlight with their deep tints; but though heavy and delicious odors intoxicated her, and lovely shapes invited her to delicate experiences in those temperate groves, there was no voice that compelled her to stay.

"Here!" whispered her lover, "let us lie here in the shadow of the camellia, and the scented snow shall descend on our bodies."

"Not here!" she answered. "Not here!"

Next she visited the tropical ferns. The moonbeams were green and gold in that moist sky; there was the silence of a fern-forest in primeval night, a stillness only broken, it seemed to her, by a faint sliding and far-off cry of some unknown thing. She was not afraid. The region was familiar, and always there attended her the vivid beauty of that flower, with whom she could take refuge if she would give up her unknown adventure. But if she could, she must be cruel to this drifting spirit who desired that she should lend him harborage and restore him for a little to the warmth and sweetness of life; she must ignore him, being under compulsion to flit and flutter from point to point like a golden moth seeking the place appointed for its mysterious dream. "Where am I to go? When will there be a change?" she asked. "The creeper climbing the walls seems to shroud the ruins of a temple," she whispered, and gazed at the pattern of small leaves against the moonlight expectantly. There was nothing, and nothing happened under the spreading fans of the tree-fern, or when she pressed her face into a feathery mass of maidenhair – except that she seemed to receive a kiss on her mouth.

"Not now," she murmured, "not now"; and hurried on through a steamy and stifling corridor of white-veined and evil plants to the lily-tank.

The stillness was more profound, the heat more oppressive, the moonlight more unearthly. Orbed and effulgent the lily floated on the water, a vessel formed out of the substance of starlight brimming with a distillation of moonbeams. In depths beneath him the world of water plants and all that tropical luxuriance of fans and blades and vivid stems was dimly redoubled. He became a star shining in the water, and as she stared into the dark universe where he swam the strange world where she was and her own golden body seemed reflected in the blackness of outer space. There was a moon-change. Among black shadows in a vast tangle of vegetation surrounding a water moved the bulks of elephants come down after the fall of night to drink, and some emerged into the moonlight, gray and ghostly; crocodiles slept under lotus leaves, lulled into savage reveries; in warm mud tortoises remembered ancient continents; there was a smooth gliding of snakes in the forest. She perceived all sounds and movements of the night with new and subtle senses; her body was responsive to the most delicate stimulations, her spirit accessible to the shyest beauty. What body was this that felt in its tissues an intermingling of the moonbeams; what mind that was appeased by a tranquillity spreading like incense from the contemplation of a flower? She was in communion with the spirit of the Water Lily.

"Flower of cold starlight!" she murmured. "Dweller in cool lakes among high mountains! What do you contemplate?"

There was an answer: "I contemplate extinction."

She had some recollection of the young man who stood at her side. She knew that beautiful, ironical face, those mystic eyes.

He was speaking. "It is not easy to contemplate extinction, within an arm's length of your beauty."

There was a story that she could only half remember; one that partly emerged, as it were, from within another. A youth . . . a poet . . . who could not obtain her. . . . She looked into his face again and saw the profound sadness of his lowered eyelids. A youth . . . a poet . . . that she had known? Another spirit, wandering through homeless time, that entreated her for the warmth of her mind? She remembered a desire.

"You will obey my wishes to-night?" Her voice wheedled him.

"If you wished for my kisses." His tones were level and melancholy. "But this singular desire . . ."

"You woke it," she said, "you, a poet. Say that you will bring me to the Lord Buddha."

"That you may marry a flower! This thought is strange."

"You conceived it," she answered, "you, a poet."

He was reluctant, but she was not to be prevented.

"You intend it, then?" He surrendered at last.

"I intend it."

"And I am no more to you than a means to enjoyment I shall not share in, a pandar?" He was white and sarcastic.

"Since it is my marriage night," she rejoined, "you may kiss me," and gave him her arms and her mouth. She knew well of the shudder that convulsed this elegant and meditative being as he obeyed her; she saw how he regained his pale, ironical self-control.

"Bravo, sovereign reason," she whispered, when he had himself in hand.

"Desire is transient," he said with a wry smile. "And in any case illusory."

"That may be," she replied, "but I will prove it for myself."

Presently there was a gondola, paddled by men whose bodies shone like dark bronze under the moon. They had eyes of night with a memory of sunset, and their foreheads were marked with the sign of a god. There began a journey, but she only heeded the end of it and had but an impression of scenes and episodes following one another swiftly and with queer caprice as in a dream. The gondola sped over the lagoon, propelled by the bronze men; they sang in the rhythm of their movements; their strength seemed

to stream like a never-ending music. The lagoon was wide sometimes, and full of glinting palm-islands; sometimes it narrowed to
a channel in a mysterious darkness of ferns. Everywhere lilies; ever
the bronze figures sang an incomprehensible song; ever the deep
eyes of her lover gazed into hers. But, "Faster! Faster!" she replied
to his silent entreaty.

They were no longer in a gondola, but driving interminably
along mounting roads, she in the disguise of a youth; and she
had impressions of white houses, dim temples, offerings of roses.
Then many changes passing in the dark of one night. "Are we not
there yet?" she constantly asked. "Shall we not come soon to the
Lord Buddha?" But her breath came faster at the thought of the
fearful excursion into vacuity that she must make.

At last the road lay through temperate forests, and for the first
time, when they descended from the ox-cart, and the young man
led her by the hand, she took sharp note of her surroundings – an
inn in a garden, a temple bright with jasmine, an image dreaming
in interior gloom, and far off the shine of Himalayan snows. But
how quiet the forest! How sweet the air! Her heart beat less wildly
in that peace; her lover's passion abated; they entered the forest
as those who are received into the fringes of a contemplation,
walking carefully, as if their movements were thoughts that might
trouble the Lord Buddha's calm. Soon they came within sight of a
place, a little way off, where golden moonbeams among the trees
were shafts of a temple containing some brighter radiance. There
was profound silence. Beast lay quiet on the grass, bird was still on
the branch, dreaming each his part within the dream of the Holy
One. Her lover held back on the threshold of that silence, gazing
somewhat wistfully as one who sees what he can never understand
or obtain, but cannot scoff.

"You still intend it?" he whispered.

"Yes," she said, emptied of all fear save the fear of that splendor.

"Alas! then farewell."

She gave him her cheek, pitiful with the Lord Buddha's pity, yet
looking sideways toward the temple of moonbeams and starlight.
She was intent on her will and scarcely felt his kisses; yet when

she found herself alone, and heard his footsteps dwindling away in the thicket, and his involuntary sobbing, she wept a little for his despair and for the sadness of the world. This the Enlightened knew and fixed his thoughts on her so that she advanced further among the trees into the circle of silence, and at last was face to face with the savior of worlds, more terrible in his serenity than wrathful deities, a heavenly Being seated in contemplation too cold for the passionate human heart. He seemed not to move, not to breathe, except as she had seen an image do when she stared at it a long time; he was more than man, more than god; but the compassion of his smile, the celestial peace of his face, took away fear. She saw in his rapt gaze darkness deeper than moonless night; because the wheel of life scarcely turned she felt a silence deeper than the silence of space; she was ready to cease, and yield herself to the hidden, omnipresent and indescribable Power whose secret she had for a moment guessed at in the Lord Buddha's eyes.

A long time passed, and she had many calm thoughts. At last a voice came from him. "What is it that you desire, thoughtful child?"

It seemed a little thing, but she told it. "I had wished to be a flower for a little while, so that I might know them, as surely you know them."

He made no answer, there was no alteration of his countenance. She forgot her wish in the contemplation of his splendor, and after a time it seemed good to her to lie down on the soft floor and share in his dream. She seemed to be once more on a journey, a ghost inquiringly roaming a night-bound region, a spirit still imprinted with human memories, flower-ghost and maiden-ghost, able, if she desired, to enter the seed of some flower and emerge with it into the experience of light and life. She wandered in a new, spacious time of her own wherever the darkness seemed fragrant with summer, putting off her choice and always saying, "In some other country the sun when he rises will be more gentle, the wind sweeter." But often she was at point to surrender her freedom because she felt intimately the sensation and experience of flowers: it might be some great beauty of dusky peonies growing in black mold, azaleas dancing on a moonlit terrace, or ivy on a wall hiding a nest of birds. Marigolds in an old garden drew her; poppies in starlit cornfields, fuchsias in a shadowy porch and crimson roses; cyclamens and magnolias on temperate and scented hillsides; starry flowers shining in the darkness of tropical forests; and blue lotuses dreaming on a night-bound water. But not only great beauties. Noisome growths drew her by contrary, and she was tempted to steep herself in the experience of poisonous plants; streaked, snaky plants; plants of an evil green with white and startling venation; ill-smelling carrion flowers; insect eaters, sticky sundews and sinister nepenthes; agaves and cactuses, fleshy, succulent and obscene; tangled and disgusting dodders, broomrapes, rusts, smuts and sickly mildews; fevers, agues and flesh-destroying poxes; parasites that prey on the living, and saprophytes that feed on the putrid dead.

"Shall I at last be the foul visitor that burrows in the substance of beauty?" she asked herself, and fled shuddering from the vision of what she might easily become.

At last the fairness and experience of a plant, one only among myriads, spoke convincingly to her; she was contented to cease wandering and give herself up to stillness and obscure dreaming.

She was on a mountain side, looking over forests to snow-peaks gleaming in starlight. It was cold, vast and beautiful as the contemplation of one who shall soon cease to be. By a little rock grew a starry flower. "Be my body, seed of this flower," she prayed, and the world faded. She was lost in a darkness, and strange and dark was the beginning of this experience: far snow-peaks fading into black forest, a lightless region of plant-forms, darkness and silence and cell blindly communicating with cell. Then all movement, all sensation, all knowledge ceasing. Then for a long time nothing.

At last, sunrise. A young flower waking to life. Dim senses, desires, satisfactions. A little stirring of the dawn-wind, and what pleasure in the compliance of the stalk! A faint tingling that increased and filled the senses with pleasure, a suffusing of all the body with golden vision, as the radiant flower of light blossomed in heaven. Hunger, thirst: a sharp, desirable moisture at

hand for refreshment. Heat, weariness: a shadow softly stealing
over when the glow of the light-flower became too ardent; scented
wind-waves bathing the longing body. Great spaces of delicious
and untranslatable sense-dreaming, while the sweetness of light
and dark alternately provoked and assuaged desires. Sometimes
a threat of invisible evils, and a shrinking of the body: sometimes
a wound, and the body swiftly renewing itself. But ever foremost,
in sensation that seemed like vision, the influence of the radiant
light-flower. At first, for many spaces, between the cool spaces of
dawn when a wind carried news from a distance, and the dark
spaces of night when delicate senses mirrored only the remote tingling of far-off and tiny light-flowers, a shrinking from that near
and dominant splendor. But soon, under insistent usage, the awak-
ening of a new and most sweet necessity. What delight, then, to
offer the body in its moment of perfection to the searching heat
of a blue-golden morning; to endure all day on the mountain side
that tenderness and that cruelty; and at last to suffer the entry of
a messenger, and resign all dreaming to the will of a remorseless
particle!

§ XXV

S HE woke lazily, the slug, with a dream that she was in some
weedy cave in the depths of a sun-irradiated sea. Then, as
the day brightened and the image of downward-sweeping leaves
of the weeping beech sharpened, she saw her golden frock, and
wondered why she was lying there with the sun drawing a pattern
on her hip. She raised her bright head and looked round. The
memory of her dream was dim in the sunshine.

She rose, and moved about inside her leaf-tent for a little while,
smelling the sweetness of the foliage that was now softly stirring,
bathing her face in the warm sun, nuzzling and peeping, a white
and gold fawn among burning leaves.

What time of day was it? Early morning, by the taste of the air.
Four o'clock? Five? It would be safe to travel in the Gardens just

now; and there was no need for the golden dress. One could run
and run, as one's limbs desired to do, in wind-light silk. Obeying
her desire for swift movement, she left her bower of beech-leaves,
crossed the rhododendron walk looking from side to side of her,
and sped through the trees. The breeze smoothed her cobweb garments against her.

She darted into the Sion vista, noted the Tropical Plant House,
now less unearthly, glistening like dew in the sunlight, and made
straight for the Lake. She desired the rush of wind, the embrace
of cold water. A breeze ruffled the surface of the Lake, and drifted
her discarded garments into a bush, where they hung like spider
webs. The water flowed coldly in her mouth and eyes, slipped
along her sides and her thighs as she struck out from the shore,
scattering a thousand diamond-drops sunward. She swam, and ran
on the grass, until it was scarcely discreet; but after her mystical
experience earthly considerations seemed to have little relevance.

Yet it was necessary to leave the Gardens, or else to hide. She
would go home, and carry the day with boldness.

Awaiting a suitable occasion, she declared herself, a couple of
hours later, to the young gardener who had looked at her so sulkily one morning earlier in the year. If anything disentangled itself
clearly from the complex of reactions that he displayed on being
confronted by this golden fragility, it was complete disbelief in her
story – a rough and ready story, for she had very rightly determined
to rely, in the case of the young gardener, on her appearance. He
was consumed, obviously, between a cynical interpretation of her
escapade, hope for himself, and a fiery belief in the good and the
beautiful inspired by the wispish delicacy of her loveliness. But he
was ready, he was eager, to lend her a mackintosh; he fell over a
barrow in his anxiety to comply with her request; and he assisted
her to put it on with an ineptitude that was highly indicative. Still
triumphant with the splendor of her experience, she would have
liked everybody to be happy. She put her hand in his, therefore,
and lightly kissed his cheek. In a year, poor man, he had pined and
died, and she regretted what she had done. But the mackintosh
was most useful to her. It enabled her to leave the Gardens with

her splendor hidden, except for the golden shoes and the glinting hair.

She walked into the morning-room, convinced of her power. They were all sitting there – her mother, Hubert, Roland – like those who wait while the coffin is being carried downstairs. Hubert, at ease in the window with his elegantly trousered legs crossed, distributing a faint aroma of pomade and expensive soap, was clearly in command. She dropped her mackintosh on the sofa.

Her mother raised her hands and gasped "Judy!" There was a trace of asthma in her gasp.

"Yes, mother?"

Her mother was pointing at her frock.

"It looks so much worse in the morning!" she exclaimed. She displayed an increasing distress. "That it should have come to this!"

Judy picked up her dress and displayed her silken legs. "Is this the token of sin?" she asked. "Is this what all the fuss is about? How odd people are, that stuffs should cause such violent and such different reactions. A man shudders at flannel; cotton stirs his imagination; and silk finally destroys his self-control. What difference is there in the chemical changes when the silk is artificial? Some one should measure it. But really, really, I don't understand."

She caught Roland's eye and felt an unexpected confusion, an odd disturbance of her nerves. He was calm, she noticed, but his calm was achieved with difficulty. She glanced at Hubert. Hubert, she felt at once, had something up his sleeve. He had ready some means with which to destroy her freedom and checkmate her plans.

"Whose is the mackintosh?" asked her brother, cool and observant.

"A friend's."

"How did you get those earth-stains on your stockings?"

"From contact with the earth."

Tears glistened on the weak, dignified and pathetic face of her mother. "Oh, Judith," she said, striving to control her emotions. "Oh, Judith. We ought never to have given you such a wicked name."

"Be quiet, mother," said Hubert, "and leave her to me."

It was hard, though salutary, for the poor lady, that she should be not only disobeyed but managed by her children.

Roland spoke. "I take it we are not going to demand explanations? Her movements are her own business."

She flashed a look of gratitude at him. This big and brown man was a friend. But she saw that all his strength was at work holding down a tempest.

"Still," he continued, "as those who are, or will be, intimately related to you, we cannot but be affected by your conduct. If you will not tell us what is going on in your mind – and we do not demand it, I beg you to remember – could you not to some extent model your behavior on what is judged reasonable, adapt yourself to what is liked?"

She desired to retain this friend, this link with a world in which for the moment she was not living; but this was an attempt to restrict her liberty. "The literary man to the life," she mocked.

"That may be." He breathed more quickly. "But I should like you to note that patience, and a desire to understand, on my side demand something more than a little smart repartee on yours."

She saw the justice of this, but she was impatient with these unnecessary discussions and only wanted to be left to her thoughts. "The repartee," she said, "will certainly be on my side."

"Then I shall have to resort to other weapons." His voice shook.

"You will fling some verbal thunderbolts, I presume?"

His calm exterior vanished. He had been too long self-controlled. "You silky, pale-eyed leopard. You slip of sarcasm. You sleek-headed torture. You luxurious tigress with your little biting teeth. Adorable beast. Darling spite. Golden tongue of hell fire!"

"Three more sentences," she cried, staring at him under a queer fascination, "and you'll win me."

"Stop it!" he cried, his muscles all instinctive to strike her. "Oh, stop it, for God's sake!"

She slipped between his arms and tempted him, remembering the arms of a lost lover, flesh of fire-containing marble. Forgetful of everything but an imagined mouth, a scented breath, she kissed

Roland, sighing, swooning, and transfixed with a sharp spear of remembered pleasure.

He tore himself away, and the door closed on him. Her heart misgave her. She had only been innocently giving herself to an experience, and why were people so concerned, so angry? Her heart certainly misgave her, for in the arms of Roland she had seemed to be supplied with something material and comforting that she lacked. Now he had flung out, with unexpected decision, and there was Hubert grinning at her from his armchair.

"I perceive," he said, "that you have an unreasonable desire for that professor. And now for the settlement of your little affair."

She braced her nerves for a contest.

The mother of these two was in tears. "You wicked, wicked girl! Oh, Hubert, what are we to do with her?" She hung on him as on hope itself.

Hubert played his card.

"We are to let her do exactly what she likes."

Judy herself was startled.

"Yes," continued Hubert, with his hands in his pockets. "She's so mad that there's money in it. That's a thing that professors don't understand, and few men of business. We must face the facts. The girl's mad, but she has something up her sleeve, and when she consents to produce it I'll put it on the market for her, at a suitable commission. I can understand people who have something to put on the market. And the first rule is – to leave them alone. You have complete liberty of movement, Judy: and if you want any help, call on me."

She would have kissed her brother, but pride forbade. She gave him one look, and dashed upstairs.

§ XXVI

O N an afternoon, late in the summer, she was walking, somewhat melancholy-minded, in the Gardens with Roland. For long now she had been moody, by turns sad and elated; but her sadness and her elation were not extreme; she lived in a summery serenity, and felt no desire for activity of any kind. While the leaves of the great trees turned a darker green, and some began to shrivel, she found in herself a tendency to reflect on the passage of time; to gaze protractedly at the deep spaces of the sky; to withdraw, at length, from the life of sensation and meditate on the nature of things through long stretches of the afternoon. This state had been easy to bring about. Day by day the composition of her mind had seemed to change, and gradually she had come to feel as if the beautiful image that walked in the name of Judith was in the possession of a stranger. What an ethereal and lovely slip she had become Roland did not fail to inform her.

A note, an apology, brought Roland back to her; a changed, reserved Roland who wooed her delicately and even (as she sometimes mockingly thought) with excess of consideration. They began again, on a basis of friendship: there were no caresses. Within him, she knew, there still burned the pain of love; but now to love there was added a sort of care, and it was agreeable to her at this time. How dear those days were that they spent in the Gardens – walking among the trees, hiding deep in some scented arbor under the temperate glass, or coolly disposed to meditation among sweet-scented shrubs – she did not tell him, except with a sort of derision; but often, in the midst of her thoughts, she would catch sight of his face, brown and intent, and she would think what changes had taken place in them both, and smile mockingly into the bushes.

Now it was towards evening, and the shadows under the cedar deepened: a touch of the darkness fell on her spirit, and she felt a vague fear. Roland observed that it was time for them to go home, and took both her hands and lifted her to her feet.

"But I can't go home," she said. "I must stay here to-night." What was it that was happening to her?

He was a little distressed. "I've seen that you are working something out in your mind. There is something clamoring for release, for expression. You don't quite know, I think, what it is. But oh, Judy, my golden dear, I can't help you."

"You are a darling," she said, "to leave me alone."

"I can't stay here with you, or near you, while you work out your problem?"

"No, oh no! But Roland, if it was over . . ."

He stared at her. "How your eyes shine in the darkness! You darling cat! Judy. . . ." He struggled with his breath. "Judy! Judy! You do not love me?"

She put her two hands against his chest. "It is possible," she whispered, "but it must be deferred." Then she put up her mouth for him to kiss her, and swiftly escaped into the shadows.

It was dark under the fans of the weeping beech, but sunset still softly flamed in the western sky. She climbed into a high fork of the tree, and sat there in the solitude and silence of evening. The Gardens were empty; she was alone; but fear had left her. There came moments of exaltation in which she mounted with the swifts and gave herself to their long fallings and wheeling flights. Higher, and she was flying, flying in regions where thought merges with the swaying of sunset-warm winds; in far, evening-bright spaces of the sky, where calm clouds, bathed in the light of hidden suns, serene spirits that have accepted the will and movement of the universe, passed across high heaven accordant to an invisible wind. Then in a long sickening moment she had fallen the whole height of the sky, and labored wingless. The sunset died out, as if all hope had withdrawn from the universe, leaving chill darkness. The darkness grew more fearful. Depths of an uncertain blackness now seemed to open before her bewildered eyes. Her mind tried to grasp at the shapes of things, and there were no shapes to grasp. She reached out for something that was stable in a world of yielding branches, unresisting leaves and fitful winds among clouds. She bruised her forehead against the branch, for the reality of pain; but she found no salvation in pain, and descended from the tree and ran through the shadowy darkness of the Gardens in anguish for the familiarity of her own room.

The familiarity of the room did not fail her; but now she found herself in another kind of despair, a kind of dullness, exhaustion and malady of spirit. "It seems unjust," she grieved, "that

this unhappy condition should be the end of a summer of glorious experiences among flowers." She wept miserably for vanished splendors. "I must quite forget them," she thought, "and be
relieved of this torture." And now she tried to achieve forgetfulness of her experiences in a sort of disintegration of the mind. But
in the minute of that painful dispersion her agony ceased. She had
no need of the Gardens, she perceived, for she herself, a flower,
was the creator of flowers. They claimed life of her mind, and she
must surrender it to them, for the time. She understood, in a blaze
of illumination, what needed to do, and slept impatiently till the
daybreak.

At the first breaking of the flushed tips of the dawn, she set herself to the board, and flowers, strange flowers she thought them,
sprang from the creative turmoil. She painted and drew all that
day, and most of the night, and several following days, watching
the curious and individual ways of her genius; thinking detached,
ordinary thoughts; eating, sometimes, and sleeping a little; but in
a rage to finish, intolerant of impediments, fierce for her children;
and day and night turned as a wheel until necessity was at an end.
Five midnights from the bitter midnight of beginning she felt that
her inspiration was satisfied, and slept in celestial peace. Her room
was a garden, bright with the flowers engendered in the flower-
like blossoming of her nature. It was a paradise, where she was
received by smiling spirits, the blessed and fortunate who have
opened their imaginations to the unknown power, and suffered
the tortures, and become parents of beauty.

Her body died. She floated like a nebula high among stars, and
had ineffable pleasures.

§ XXVII

SHE woke, in a cold and silvery daybreak at the end of summer,
to a world that perhaps no longer contained anything to set
her heart on with undue desire; for she had seen what the mind
fumbles after, what the senses only half tell, and until that strange

agitation should return, with its delicious accomplishment, who should lead her to more than fugitive delights? There was nothing to love or loathe out of measure – thus her thoughts ran during a day of restful meditation.

In the afternoon, a sad afternoon of late summer, when the spirit knows that but a few more days of the authentic splendor shall return before the advent of the year's evening, her thoughts were interrupted by Hubert, who knocked respectfully at the door. She was quite ready for the world, now, and answered, "Come in." He entered on tiptoe, and indeed the world entered with him, and the states of mind she had known in the summer now seemed very far away.

"It's all right," she said. "The fit's over."

"Ah!" His air changed. The respect for her productive privacy that he had shown during the last few days was no longer needed: but there was a perceptible increment of deference in his manner – was she not now a client? He looked anxiously at her drawings; but his anxiety was at once relieved, for with swift judgment he perceived that the obtainable sterling equivalent of the goods was considerable. "It will need a large expenditure to create the necessary fuss about them," he said, with the glad voice of one who has the first option on a good thing; "but it can be done. They are queer, you see."

"Not exactly representational art," she replied.

"But there is something that sticks out of them – I don't mind admitting it. Though for the life of me I can't say what. We shall have to get some highbrow to write something. Is it a deal?"

"What are you going to charge me?"

"Ten per cent., as you're my sister."

"I'll let you have it," she said, "as you're my brother."

He grinned.

"You don't mind my being a little mad, now?" she inquired.

"Nothing is mad that results in financial advantage."

"But what do you say, now, about my being economically independent?"

"You're not economically independent. You're dependent on me."

"I really feel," she admitted, "that part of my success will be due to you."

"Practically all of it," he answered.

"Did you guess what was happening from the first?"

"Yes. And as soon as I was certain of it I cleared the way for you, with the results we see around us. I am always right."

"Well, advise me again," she begged. "Ought I to marry Roland?"

"Yes, if you can't marry some one like me."

"I think I would," she said, "if you were not my brother. For your common sense no longer has any terrors for me. In fact, I rather like it, and you know your way about."

"I will admit," he said handsomely, "that I do not altogether understand what goes on in your mind. But I can see that you have experiences that are important to you, and fortunately productive."

"And you still advise me to marry?"

"It cannot do any harm."

"And to marry Roland?"

"I take it he will do as well as any one?"

"Better," she said, with cheeks burning. "He rather pleases me."

"Oh, it's like that, is it?" said Hubert, obviously detecting her secret. "An odd thing, a habit. One gets to think one is fond of people. I really came up to tell you that he's waiting downstairs now."

"Let him come in five minutes. He must see my flowers." Her heart thumped; she put on a cornflower-blue frock, and brushed her yellow hair with the tortoiseshell brush. "Have I changed?" she asked of her image in the long mirror. "Has this alteration that I feel so strongly inside me had any effect on my exterior?" But it was the same tow-headed Judy that stared at her with eyes of a mysterious light gray. She touched her lips with paint and shook her frock into place with a wriggle. "It's the sense of the world coming back to me," she told herself. "I feel it. I shall encourage it." But at a glimpse of the pale and pictured sky her heart was smitten with the grief of a remembered music.

When Roland came in, however, she did not beat about the

bush, and kissed him as if she acknowledged all rights. Roland, on his part, did not press them. He did indeed take her to the window-seat and adequately demonstrate his joy.

"Oh, that was actual!" she exclaimed. "There was something comforting in the reality of that!" But she perceived that he was not listening.

"Flowers!" she heard him say.

He left her side and made his inspection.

"What do you think of them?"

"Large as life," he said, smiling. "And much less natural. I told you once that poets can make effects with words that quite eclipse anything in nature. Thus you. You are a poet and artist. Reality, call it what you like, looks out of these flowers. A matter of rela-tionships, proportions . . . synthetic power . . . rhythmic vitality . . . There are so many words. Literature, perhaps, cannot achieve what painters and musicians can achieve. I have tried. It has at any rate given me understanding."

They were silent for a long time, and the evening seemed to be sad with a sadness in his voice. Afternoon had waned, the day was going westward with ashen torches, the trees were turning silver under pallid and remote skies. A wisp of smoke curled up from a fire in the garden where already some fallen leaves were heaped, and some dead flowers, shriveled and pitiful beside the living glories of late summer – dahlias, hollyhocks, sunflowers, and all that appear when the splendor of the year is full, and coming soon to decay. Now, as she meditated on the burning, and memories of June floated away like smoke into the empty air, the garden became crowded with a bodiless and memorial throng; it seemed to her that a prince, dead in the flesh and now but a ghost in her imagination, was laid on the pyre; and she thought, if she strained her attention, that she heard a sad and heavenly music, such as fills the heart with desire for the peace of death and the glory of unseen things. Clearly she saw the form of that vanished Flower, laid on the pyre, and she was wrung, looking out safely from the arms of her lover, by a remembrance of his splendor and pride and eagerness in life. The pyre burned brightly, and now his memory fled to the formless expanses of heaven on flames that grew in the pure and evening air in the ghostly resemblance of petals of bright flowers. Not many mourned for the dead, for the many get but little advantage from even the most passionate and beautiful of tragic lives; but they grieved, such as love to be moved by sad occasions, for pity of their own doom. Presently faint words were stirring in the air, and there reached her the fading voice of a pale, meditative ghost. In vain she resisted the voice.

"How shall I capture the myriad beautiful griefs that flutter on my spirit like wings of birds, plaintive birds, wheeling and skimming in this silvery and mournful evening of the summer's end? The dead have faded before ourselves into the lightless regions. They have given us a foretaste of the bitterness of oblivion, and enabled us to feel the grief of our own decease. Life is short, splendid and beautiful sunflowers. It is a brief opening to the glory of light, a swift closing and return into decomposition. This is a mystery – that the immense processes of the universe, the ponderous integration of diffused particles, the reduction of ethereal space through ages of time to reproductive matter, the slow invertebration of mud and delicate contrivance of vegetables, should end merely in the opening of a flower, the brief anguish of consciousness. Life has nothing more treasurable, glorious geraniums, beautiful asters, than the grief of living; the most valuable moment of existence is that moment when we perceive the sadness of having been. Only eternity is kind, for it is forgetfulness, and in it all flowers and all existence vanish. The evening cloud has a golden light on it, and presently it changes, and soon there is only the emptiness of space, the silence of nothing, the memory of us is gone. . . ."

The waves of his words died away, and a chill wind of the silver dusk stirred so that the flowers shivered, and the flame-petals of the pyre shrank from it. She, too, shivered and suddenly turned to her lover for protection, shutting out mysteries and the summons of strange beauty, until her spirit should have been a little renewed.

"Let us shut the window," she said. "It's cold. And it is senseless, irrelevant, all this talk of life and death."

"I heard no talk," he said, "but I understood that you had a vision. You were very quiet, and now there are tears on your eyelids, tiny crystals with a gleam of sunset."

"I give them to you. Taste them."

He kissed her eyelids. "Do you indeed love me?" he asked.

"Yes! Oh yes! I love you, and you are real. Hold me while I tell you something."

He held her fast. "You have learnt me," she said, "and you know, perhaps, how to handle me. You know, don't you, that I can't always be in love?"

He nodded. "I know, and it doesn't matter."

"And that sometimes you mustn't even try to awaken me?"

"I may sometimes make mistakes." He seemed a little bewildered. "Trial and error, you know."

"But at the present minute . . ." She closed her eyes on the last gleam of daylight in the shimmering blue of the walls, and offered her mouth. For the time being the ghosts were laid.

THE END